Looking for the Last Piece

Bernadette Warren

Fisher King Publishing

For Miriam, in case I'm not here to tell you where the stars come from. With love from your Nannan on the day of your birth. Welcome to the world. xxx.

To (in order of appearance): Her Royal Highness after the God of Single Combat, Law and Justice.

She who is Industrious, striving and excels and He who is honoured by God.

She who lived Nobly, The Lioness of God who is the Answered Prayer, The Honeyed one, The Star of the Sea and The Ewe.

Gift of God, The Dwellers by the rushes, God is gracious. She who is clean and pure and People's victory.

The Princess. She who is the Ever Youthful Jupiterian and He who is Noble.

The Characterful Goddess of War, Wisdom, Grace and Peace.

He whom God remembers, and the Earth Worker. The Hardy Ruler. The Dweller at the top of the meadow, and The Pure White willow

With the most deep and fondest Gratitude to the above, which because of their support and vision, these tales have been released.

I love you.

May The Divine Assistance remain with you
ALWAYS.

Many moons and skies ago,

The Earth turned and Watched life grow.

The Sun its light it spread for free,

The days were long, and all were happy.

But come the night, the darkness spreading overhead,

It's blanket deadening laughter and song,

Sometimes for much too long.

Until one morning,

The Sun shook the sand from his eyes,

Looked at the Earth and asked

"Why do you cry?"

The Earth looked across and at once replied,

"The Moon is sad when you are on the other side.

And tho' we see you shining on her face,

Space at night is a lonely place.

Because you are so far away,

She'd like some friends to come and stay."

The Sun looked for a clue to lead the way to a happy

Moon.

So,

He swam through a spinney,

Out over a lake

And there

Shining,

Was the perfect path to take.

The Sun spoke to the Wind,

Who in turn called the

Rain

To drop in.

The Sprites and the Damselflies had a bit of a chat.
A plan was set,
That was that.
The Sprites brought silver and gold from the lakebed
Up to the top
For the Damselflies to rake,
Skimming the shimmering stuff from the surface
Into special jars
For the Faeries to take
Up to the Moon
To flood the Sky with Stars.
Now she has company Through the long hours.
So
If you look And listen long
When the Moon is fat,
You will see her beaming face,
Singing,
Happy,
Just Like
Thaaaaaaat!

CHAPTER ONE

Late 1800s

Ireland

John Kennedy grew up with the Ashton brothers. They were once close, but the scales of their friendship began to tip when Mary O'Sullivan turned Thomas's head. The Ashton brothers, Thomas, Peter and Joseph, and the O'Sullivan sisters, Mary, Anne and Badb, became a tight unit. They included John in everything, but the sisters did not think like him. The Blacksmith, who trained and employed Thomas, died. His widow sold the forge to Thomas and his brothers. Eight seasons later, Thomas proposed to Mary.

Not to be left behind, John decided that he too would marry an O'Sullivan. Badb, just of age to marry, was too opinionated, and was too old to be tamed and put in her place. Because Anne appeared malleable, was purposeful, kept her head down and rarely said anything untoward, was kind, thoughtful and could cook, she was the obvious choice. He proposed in the orchard. Badb was up a tree at the time, and he felt humiliated when Anne gently declined the offer of a better life as a Kennedy in England.

To prove Anne wanting in her refusal, John moved to Belfast, where he found clerical work with the law, courtesy of Mr. Peel.

John Kennedy was coming to terms with inheriting nothing, while Harry, his much older cousin, was bequeathed their paternal grandfather's estate in entirety. As consolation, Harry bought John a new suit, and took him on a pub crawl in Dublin.

In a tavern, where a group of Irish soldiers were on a last shout before their volunteered service with the British Army at The Second Boer War, the atmosphere was congenial; not the scene of excitement that Harry was expecting from John's description. Aware of Harry's growing impatience with the cordiality, and eager to impress his English born cousin who lived a life which he aspired to, John disparagingly pointed out two men from his hometown of Clontarf, a backwater nearby. One man was employed in flattering the landlady at the bar, the other by the piano, serenading Ireland's grace to a hushed and teary saloon. Harry sprinkled a little pepper into the pot.

"Your friend, the canary over there. He thinks well of himself for not fighting for his own birth right and giving his soul to kill for the British Heathens. Someone needs to order the shite to take that uniform off."

John agreed. "He's no friend of mine; he's too thick with the O'Sullivans."

"All the more reason to show him who's boss."

"He may not look much, but believe me, it needs a clever man to do it. I would, but I don't want to crease my new suit."

"Well look at you Johnny, all sounding like a man.

You can take him. You're a Kennedy like me; the man deserves to be put on his arse, but if you're not up for it, we may as well get to our beds."

John was unsure.

The strains from the Irish Tenor faded, and John decided that it might be a good idea to order the Singing Soldier, to remove the uniform he was proudly wearing after all. Full of false courage as appreciation for the finished song grew, John stood behind the soldier. A tray with two glasses of stout floated over the crowd for the entertainers. It narrowly missed John's head, and was placed without spilling a drop, next to the soldier's hat on the piano top. John drew a deep breath, puffed out his chest, and tried to square his sloping puny shoulders. John's naivety about his size was a great tool for Harry's fun. The applause cooled as John blarted out the order.

"Hey, Taig. I think you should remove the weeds of the country you're protecting and expanding, the Empiric rapists of the Homeland you sing for before you desert." John looked around the room and caught Harry's wink of encouragement and pressed on. "Before I make you."

Harry felt tremors of excitement rise in his stomach.

The soldier smiled and handed the stout to the pianist.

John was ignored. He looked to Harry for an encouraging nod. The soldier swallowed the thick Guinness in seconds, and John prodded the soldier on his back. All eyes were on the soldier, and all ears were waiting in the deathly silence of the pub for his retort; the landlady removed everything from the bar top.

John flinched as the soldier turned to face his audience, narrowing his eyes at John's stiffened finger, ready to prod again. A gasp or two relayed around the room, and John cowered below the soldier's raised empty glass and his toast to Ireland.

"Erin go Bragh."

As the crowd responded with like, the soldier put his Slouch Hat at a jaunt on his head and leaving John's dignity almost intact, he departed. His friend was still at the bar, too busy to notice anything other than the landlady's cleavage. Harry's ploy to see fireworks that night had failed. However, John, with money rattling in the pockets of his brand-new pants and the grog fuzzing his brain, had other ideas.

Harry returned from the bar with a whisky for himself, John was nowhere to be seen. Someone shouted that six against one was about to kick off in the alley outside, and that John Kennedy was threatening the soldier with a pistol; the room cleared. Harry felt inside his jacket. His stupid cousin had lifted his gun. Maybe his firework wasn't a damp squib, and there was to be a display after all. Harry patted his breast pocket. The treasure he carried in it was still there. He swallowed his drink and found a good viewpoint under a streetlamp outside and made himself comfortable.

John's Anglophobic friends moved forward in support, and the soldier's company, fewer in number, but burlier, made ready just in case. The soldier's friend, no longer attending to the landlady was on the pub steps, waiting for his cue.

John shouted, so those at the back could hear. "I'll give you one more opportunity to remove that emblem you wear, or you won't have to wait for a foreigner to snuff you. I'll do you myself for your disloyalty."

John's target was aware that everyone was waiting for him to throw the first punch, but he was not going to give the drunkard in front of him, or the crowd, the satisfaction of seeing any sport that night. Things were different now. He and Vincent O'Sullivan were going to see the world, courtesy of the British Army.

"Away on the road with you Johnny. You're all puffed up like a courting pigeon, and as I don't want your feathers on my wool, I'll bid you a good night." John put his arm on the soldier's chest in attempt to prevent his departure.

At first there was not much to see, but everyone at the back of the crowd, heard a cry in pain as the soldier's wit and single upper cut, lay John out on the floor. Vincent and his friend walked away from the melee which ensued and headed for bed on the last night on their Mother Country.

The brawl rolled in Harry's direction, so he decided to lend a hand. A few right hooks and skull breakers later, a couple of youths jumped Harry, and he felt suddenly weaker. A searing blow across the back of his head sent him to the floor. He felt for the treasure in his breast pocket, but it had gone. After the crowd had limped home for the night, Harry and John combed the area for the lost piece, but it was not to be found. Blaming John for the opportune Finger Smith who had lifted it from his pocket, Harry went back to England, to the business of gaining control of his maternal grandfather's small holdings in Yorkshire.

In Northern England

Aged eighteen, a fine horseman, bare-chested and athletic, Jack Raven had 'grabbed' his wife at the meet in Appleby. Elizabeth, a pale complexioned redhead, fifteen years of age, was thoroughly flattered by the attentions of the burly Jack. He promised Elizabeth that they would soon enjoy the life of luxury that the three of them surely deserved.

Two winters further along the road, Elizabeth Raven had suffered yet another miscarriage and woe betide anyone who got in Jack's way this night. Jack was bored of everything. The only life his gene had known was the road, the freedom, fresh air, the abuse from gorgers who didn't know the difference between Romani and pikey. He had grown tired of it. Things were going to change. He went to the village to buy ale.

Standing by the hatch at the inn on the crossroads in Ganche Lin, Jack noticed a trail of white pipe smoke rising from a high-backed settle by the hearth of the inglenook. Although the smoker could not see Jack, he recognised the tone of distress, anger and weakness in the voice of the gypsy at the hatch. He had ordered two tankards, quickly followed by another two as soon as the first one had hit the bar top empty.

The smoker smiled to himself. Here was a man with needs. When a person's needs became desperate, they would always prove to be of use to him. He left the hearth, paid for the ale and invited Jack to sit by the fire with him. At first Jack had refused but the ale smelled good, and now the man was walking back to the hearth with a jug of whisky in his other hand. Peter, Jack's younger brother, was with Elizabeth should the laudanum wear off. "You look like you could do with an ear. Call me Harry, if you like."

Jack warmed his hands in front of the fire and listened to Harry telling him about his dreams and fears. He wanted to leave but he was too caught up with everything the man said. News travelled fast through small towns and villages, and this man knew more than Jack was happy with. Jack prepared to thump him if he said anything else. "No need to thank me Jack. This is what friends do." Jack stumbled back to camp with Harry's voice in his head and tried to remember what he was thanking his new friend for.

Jack Raven's character had been just as dubious as the Anglican bishop and the prominent local MP with whom he loosely associated at the time. They all had habits and tastes which, had they been revealed, would at the very least be deemed insalubrious and at the worst thoroughly damning. However, theirs would be the only careers that would be put at risk should it come to public light and

Jack knew this. The knowledge was a perfect fulcrum that would one day lever Jack onto a vast medieval abbey estate owned by the High Anglican Church.

Now in a position to commission Raven's Court, Jack used designs stolen from a young Lutyens before he had gone on to become an established architect. The Arts and Crafts red brick Tudor-style country house with five chimneys was completed in the late 19th century. Jack swapped horse trading for the more lucrative sheep farming throughout York, Malton and Ganche Lin. Five years and three miscarriages later, Jack had lifted both himself and his brother Peter from the humble Romanichal in which they had been born. He was determined to enjoy a piece of the cake that was eaten by few and dreamed of by more.

As the sheep trading quickly developed, Jack employed Arthur McArthur as his chief shepherd. One Sunday when he should have been deep in prayer at mass, Arthur smiled shyly at the personal maid of the soon-to- become Lady Raven. Frances Lamb became Frances McArthur, and they set up home in a crumbling one up one down cottage on the estate for a nominal peppercorn rent.

Early 20th Century

Harry's parents and those of his maternal cousin, Marian the favourite, were now dead. Harry, with his new qualifications in law, was assisting his illiterate and failing maternal grandfather, in writing his last will and testament.

In Yorkshire, all was well above Ganche Lin, until the Irishman named Vincent O'Sullivan appeared on the hill and scuppered Harry's plans with his charm, muscle, and surprising intelligence for what he called a Mick. From the beginning, Harry saw something familiar in the newcomer's face, but now, the familiar ring in the air, the determination to repossess something he believed to be gone forever, placed the now older profile before him. He remembered the scene in the Dublin pub with John. Vincent had not taken it. He and the other soldier had left the scene before it was stolen, unless he was in on the theft.

Harry's chest was full of determination to relieve the newcomer of the piece. Despite attempts to stifle the interloper's progress, Vincent thrived. He bought the ruined castle at the top of the hill from Harry and Marian's grandfather and built his new house around it. When permission was given for Vincent to marry Marian, Vincent paid a visit back to Ireland to give the good news.

Harry gave up his plans for his maternal grandfather's properties, paltry by comparison to what he would secure with the piece in his possession again. He scoured Vincent's house until Marian, unwittingly informed him that Vincent kept the piece of metal about his person. Harry pondered on which lacky he could count on to help him secure it on Vincent's return; it did not take long. He paid a call on Jack Raven.

A fleeting ring caused Thomas Ashton to look up from honing the shears he had forged in his small foundry on the outskirts of Clontarf. Through the open doors he spied Vincent O'Sullivan approaching along the track. When Vincent landed in England, after the fight over gold in Africa in the Second Boer War, he had considered Ireland, but his maternal relations disowned him for joining the British Army. This banishment raised no problem.

Vincent had found his own crock of gold, in Yorkshire, and said that he would never put foot on Ireland again. His recent letter, informing Thomas of his forthcoming secret visit, was a pleasant yet a total surprise. Calling out, Thomas set off to greet him.

"Have you changed your mind, and decided to come back after all? Has Bill come back with you?"

"Keep it down Thom. He'd like to, but no, he hasn't. I doubt he will since the last fight he had the day before we left."

"It was a long time coming. The seat of John's pride is still as sore as when Bill put him on it."

"Besides, the Rudd's are a funny bunch and like many others who took a chance, family blood is thin with shame, rather than flowing thick with relief and pride we're still alive when so many snuffed it."

"Bill's intuition was always spot on! he'll not be welcomed back. I'll shout Badb down from the Orchard. She's missed her cousin The Hero, but prepare yourself, she's taller, and her head and mouth are bigger."

"No Thom. Don't call her. Nobody knows that I am back yet. I had to come here first. Keep it quiet Thomas."

"Keep it quiet? They probably knew that you were

coming before you did yourself."

Vincent hung a bag over the nose of the anvil.

"I know you've just arrived from the boat as it were, but how long are you staying?"

"As long as it takes to soften the soil."

"Well by the look of your luggage Vincent, you may need more clothes for your task with your kin."

"Look in the bag."

Thomas picked open the bag and took out a box. In the box, a leather pouch rested on rock salt. He waved the pouch at Vincent, who nodded at Thomas to open it. The pouch contained a piece of metal, about three inches wide as long, almost flat, and surprisingly sharp at the bevelled edges. Usually, one piece of metal from a broken weapon was much like another, but this piece held history. Its vibrations made Thomas's big gnarly hands feel soothed and warm. His face glowed.

"Do you know what you're holding?"

"Yes. It's Wootz steel. Indian, but possibly Roman, a fine archaeological find. My hands are tingling. How did you come by it?"

"A man gave it to me. Well, he threw it at me as if it burned his hands. He said he had been following us, hiding himself within the company, waiting for the right person who would know how to handle and look after it; he needed to get rid of it."

"Don't tell me. He had stolen it, and the person he stole it from, stole it before that and met a gruesome end not long after it left his possession."

"In a nutshell. I tried to give it back, but he wouldn't let me. He told me to hide it safely. All the while, he was looking over his shoulder, as if he were being followed. We never saw him again after that.

"The piece you have slipped into your pocket, which you call Wootz, dates back to the Crucifixion."

Thomas played with the piece of metal. Suddenly giddy, playful, he chuckled like a child.

"Another relic! If all the pieces of the Holy Cross were piled up, they would reach higher than Carrauntoohil. Did you mention it in your letters? Although artefacts in England can bring good money, I doubt this is worth anything."

"And your father a Clergyman. I'm serious Thomas, this isn't a game."

"I can tell by your tone Vin, but I thought your Holy Father sits over that one under the Basilica. Vincent, I know the O'Sullivans are a superstitious bunch, but I thought you were a bit more level-headed. How much of your hard-earned punts did it cost you for the story Vin?"

"Me and my money are not parted easily. I told you."

"And you want to own it Vin?"

"No, although I don't know where I have to take it. But apparently, piece finds piece finds Peace."

"Your part is to gather all the pieces?"

"I bloody hope not. My name means conquering, but my days of fighting are over Matey. All I know, is that I must keep it safe, and I know no one else better to help me. Can you smelt it Thom?"

"I can do that for sure Vincent, but why? It is rather fine to hold."

Mary called out. Breakfast was ready.

"Come into the house. Mary still brings enough for the unexpected guest. We will discuss it over food."

"There is no time. I'm away to the maiden aunts for an ear bashing after here."

"Well, the best way to hide your piece of straw, is in a stack. How long do I have?"

"Home is now on a hill above a village called Ganche Lin, in Yorkshire. I'm going back as soon as I can.

Around the table on the last night of his visit, the O'Sullivans and the Ashtons shared good wine, a roast lamb dinner and the coffee Vincent had brought from Taylors in York. Vincent spoke of his intentions to marry Marian.

"You're telling me that you're going to marry a Kennedy? Have you finally gone bonkers?"

"You should listen more with your ears than your imagination Badb. Marian is the blood relation of the wife of John Kennedy's uncle. She's a Nice, not a Kennedy."

"Anybody's nicer than a Kennedy! God Vin, your English is poor these days."

"Very funny; well, it would be if John's cousin Harry were not so controlling and intrusive. I believe that I have spoiled his plans somewhat, and he would rather see me off the hill."

"Everybody loves you Vin. Are you sure?"

"I'm telling you Mary, not everybody has your heart

girl. I arrived on the hill, started things moving on Marian's failing family homestead and things began looking up. I only realised the connection when Harry returned from his travels. By then, the first part of our house was tied into the castle ruins, and the Bans were out. I tell you, if Barabbas lived today, he'd die in prison."

"Meaning what?"

"Meaning, that how I live speaks louder than Harry's attempts to besmirch my reputation with the small communities on the hill, and in the village of Ganche Lin. When the house was finished, I caught him watching me looking over the piece. He's a collector of old stuff. He tried to buy it a few times, and he's offered me good amounts of money for it. So that blows your 'it's not worth anything' theory Thom. Anyhow, he wants what I have."

"It's just a bit of metal. What's the nag? You could've made a punt or two." Thomas was about to explain, but Vincent cut in.

"It's not about money Badb."

"I'm going to miss you terribly Vin."

"Remember Baddy, soon comes quicker than you think. We'll all be together then."

Early the next morning, swathed in the warmth and affection of the sisters, Vincent left his cousins' house. He reached the foundry as Thomas was laying his work out on a bench.

"You're a clever man. If I didn't know mine so well Thomas, I wouldn't spot it."

A moment later, Badb's steps crunched towards them. Vincent raised his arm and Badb sank under the weight of it as it closed around her.

"Haven't you got work to do Badb?"

"I have, but it will still be there when you're on the water. I couldn't wait for soon to become now. Mary's on the hunt, I can't be long." Badb pulled the small silver bell from side to side on the chain around her neck and glanced over Thomas's work.

"They're very beautiful. Aren't you going to initial your work Thomas?"

"Why the need?"

"They're almost identical. I take it that the other is for your Maid Marian Vin. It's a lovely gift."

Vincent took his arm from Badb's shoulder and looked at Thomas, who was trying to curb his indignance.

"What do you mean almost? Point out the difference, you cheeky mare."

"It's no slight on your workmanship Thom, don't drop your pinny. I can't explain it, but I bet I could find the original one blindfold."

Putting her to the test, they shuffled the pieces to the other end of the bench. True to her word, Badb found the original.

"Now your turn Vin." Vincent picked the wrong one. "Y'see. You should know by now cousin."

They heard Mary singing out for Badb. Vincent and Thomas cringed under the loudness of Badb's reply.

"I'm Coming! I'd better go, I've got to milk the goats.

We'll be seeing you, I'm sure." Mary's singing segued to shouting. "There she goes again! Alright Mary! Loosen your wait!"

Thomas wrapped one of the pieces and handed it to Vincent.

"No Thomas, this is safer here with you, until I know where to put it."

"Whatever you say, but it has saved your life, and others. I thought that it was your Talisman."

"I'll carry the original. To be honest, I feel safer with it here. If it is what the man who threw it at me said it was, no way on God's Earth, should Harry get his mitts on it; he's bad enough as it is."

Back in England, on realising that Vincent had returned without the piece, it was outrage which filled Harry's chest.

Vincent married the love he had found on a hill above the village of Ganche Lin.

Aware of the artefact which Harry said that he found on an archaeological dig at a Crusade battle ground when he was a student, and ever more determined to cross the water as bad times swept through Ireland yet again, John began ingratiating himself into Harry's favour. As more of Irelands population fled disease and poverty, many who stayed succumbed. The Norse Men who landed on the soil in 795AD held more respect for the body and spirit of the peoples of Ireland, than the latest natural and political invasions. As before, The O'Sullivans were riding Mother Nature's onslaughts. Their small holding and linen crops thrived, as did Thomas and his brothers with their forge. Was it miracle after miracle that kept their homestead and the foundry going? Or was it other means unseen? Witchcraft was still an arrestable offence.

John's envy, developed into ambition. He suggested, in light of Vincent's secret visit, that Thomas, or the sisters might be aware of the piece, and he was very happy to assist in the quest to have it returned. John dug around into the sisters' affairs and told Harry that he knew of the object's whereabouts.

Harry responded with an offer to cross the Irish Sea, to a better life in England. With a job in the legal profession, and a better income to enjoy, he was going to get that which Harry said he deserved. The O'Sullivans were looked into, checked over, and thoroughly audited, but John's action failed. He tried again, this time convincing the powers in Belfast, to issue a warrant for the arrest of the O'Sullivan women, on the grounds of Witchcraft. Thomas would surely pay the ransom with Vincent's possession.

Word quickly spread and the O'Sullivan sisters were able to avoid arrest. At short notice, they relinquished their lives in Ireland, Badb, disguised as a boy, was the first to go.

With the shock of seeing their little sister looking like their cousin Vincent as a boy, Mary and Ann, relieved Badb of her bundle of possessions, then they left her in the scullery to prepare themselves for their staggered exodus.

Thomas shouted. "Mary! Baddy's bindings are coming loose. There's a bulge. Better sort it out. The Crows are crying sundown." Mary crunched Badb's chest, but the bulge remained.

Thomas held the jacket open and pulled Badb's jewellery from the inside pocket. He lectured her for a second, then he handed the jewellery to Mary, who put it in a pocket in the carpet bag on the table.

"Don't worry Love, it will be around your neck again soon."

Thomas followed Mary out of the scullery, and Badb quickly found what she was looking for in Mary's bag. Each of the sisters had an identical piece. Their grandfather had three made by the blacksmith, when Badb was born, and they had carried them ever since. It made her feel safe. Badb pulled at her shirt and fed the small silver bell on a chain into the bindings, so lovingly wrapped around her by Mary and Anne. She tightened the belt around the high-waist trousers as Thomas and Mary returned, then she left them to say their goodbyes and she climbed onto the cart.

It was dark when they reached the docks in Belfast, and Thomas felt safe enough to leave Badb with the cart for a few minutes. When he returned, John Kennedy was standing beside the cart. He was looking pleased with himself.

"Now, Thomas, isn't it a bit late for you both? Shouldn't you be by your fire, or in your bed at this dark hour?"

"No more than any other fool who has to get their hands dirty John. I'll be away to meet my cousin then. Sailed in this afternoon from Liverpool. Family business."

As Thomas drove the horse away, John spotted something moving under the canvas over the wagon bed. John's Barney stick slipped around in his hand, lubricated by the sweaty mix of fear and excitement running down his arm and blending with grease of the day. Fear, because when Harry discovered that he had the piece, but had sailed West instead of East, his bridges would be burnt. But with the piece, he need never be grateful, or answer to anybody again, so what would it matter. He scurried off in the other direction.

Thomas and Badb climbed down from the cart as Joseph walked down the Gangway. Badb and Joseph swapped jackets.

"What's this on my jacket Badb?"

"Good to see you too Joseph. Blame your brother for the snail trails on your sleeve and the smell of vomit."

"Are you coming down with something Baddy? You sound like you swallowed the dust in the drizzle on your ride?"

"You can blame that on your brother too. I doubt I'll ever sing again."

Thomas hissed, "Hush your tongues y'idiots You never know where the Devil's hiding. Come on now we must be swift." He handed a bag containing a box to Badb. "This is for Vincent. Do not take it from its wrapping Badb! I know your curiosity; you must keep it hidden."

Badb held the pouch tight under one arm, and her other arm instinctively made for Thomas's neck.

"I suppose this is it then Thom?" Thomas stepped back, shook her hand vigorously and slapped her hard on her shoulder, the usual public farewell with his brothers. Joseph gave her the same treatment, then he climbed under the canvas covering the wagon. Thomas noticed Steven twitch. They had purposely left boarding until the very last moment, but the wind and the tide were turning.

"Now get on. Keep God in your pocket."

"Always Thom. And the same to you."

Steven escorted Badb to her cabin, and Thomas walked his horses away from the dock side.

Behind them, the fret that swam and floated around the bollards, punts and jetties, pulled away with the tide, taking Badb safely aboard Steven's Scotland bound boat, and the onward two-day journey to Yorkshire. Once she felt the movement of the boat, Badb rummaged inside the bindings around her waist. She let the weight of the bell ripple and pool the silver chain hand to hand through her fingers.

John was heading in Thomas's direction again, but this time, with the muscle of the Militia for company. John, despite his schooling could not parry the thrust of Thomas's logic and veiled sarcasm, and each counter-punch made him wince. He threw a warrant for the arrest of the O'Sullivans at Thomas. Laughing, Thomas handed the warrant back.

"Have we gone back to 1711 Islandmagee? Now, I

have no way of knowing exactly what they are doing, my friend of many years."

"Your wagon is looking a bit full Thomas."

Thomas took the whip from its holder, then he leant forward in a manner which John Kennedy decided to be threatening. Finally, he was able to make Thomas pay for his insolence over the years. He signalled to the Militia. Two of the men stabbed the canvas that covered the wagon with their bayonets, until a voice cried out obscenities into the night.

Swearing in Gaelic, snarling and yawning in sync with Thomas's Irish wolfhound, Joseph climbed onto the bench at the front of the wagon. He picked at his ripped trousers and rubbed his leg, grazed by one of the blades. Grinning, Thomas chided his brother in English,

"Now, Joseph, is that any way to speak to these peaceful people looking for trouble where there is none to be found?"

Leaning forward, elbows on his knees, Joseph pulled his collar up and his hat down while muttering a warning in Gaelic from under the peak of his cap.

"Trouble will come if they try to tickle me with their blades again brother. It's a dark moon. Who does he think he is, and we are? It's no wonder he's afraid of the dark."

The exchange continued in their Mother Tongue

"I've no idea Joseph. Some people are too willing to forget their roots, forge false loyalties, and fail to recognise and celebrate differences. Is Peter away in the west?"

"Aye."

John Kennedy hated all that was his heritage, but although he had forgotten most of his native tongue, he recognised a little. He ordered one of the Militias to send a messenger to the West Coast. After the brothers had re-loaded and covered the wagon, they climbed up onto the bench. They were still conversing in Gaelic. Thomas called softly to the hound, and it trotted back, sniffing around the legs of the militia before leaping up to sit behind the brothers. Thomas addressed his former friend with a genuine wish, which John understood, but let fall.

Thomas cracked his five-foot whip in the air above the horses, riffling John's hair as the fly whizzed past his head. The horses pulled the wagon in the welcome direction of home.

Badb was too sick on the crossing to be curious about the parcel she was carrying and had forgotten all about it until Vincent met her at Malton station.

"Give me a chance to park my cheeks beside you before you grill me Vin. No, my curiosity did not get the better of me. Thomas was very particular in his instruction, so yes, your bayonet is still wrapped up." Vincent's horses pulled the cart home, and the cousins caught up.

"So, you see Baddy, Marian's cousin, is to be avoided whenever possible. Watch your step. Remember, he's related to that Crapcan back in Belfast who got too big for his boots. They're all the same."

A few days later as he reached the top of a newly scrubbed staircase, Badb met Harry. He was feigning remorse for kicking the pailful of dirty water across the hall and giving the maid more work to do. He walked past Badb and stopped for a moment but did not turn. When a droning vibration drew a fearful tug at her stomach, Badb felt for the bell underneath her blouse; the drone ceased, and the fear left her. Taking note of the vibrations emanating from Badb, Harry decided to go back down the stairs. A week later in Belfast, John picked his letter off the hall stand and left his lodgings. Instead of walking through another drizzly morning to work, he caught the horse drawn tram, and read his letter from Harry.

'My Cousin. At last, despite not having secured the O'Sullivan sisters, nor my piece, I believe that getting what you deserve is long overdue. Please find enclosed, as promised, your ticket to cross over, and never go back. Be careful now Johnny.'

John Kennedy swaggered into the police station and informed the Chief that he was leaving the force because of their ingratitude, and its prejudices which refused him any advancement. The English Chief Inspector raised his head for a moment and said goodbye. John waited for a little more acknowledgement, but none came.

He was to sail the following night. He packed one bag, then he left his history behind him. Two days after John Kennedy was said to have emigrated to America, a man was found floating face-down between the punts at the docks. His skull and face were beaten beyond recognition by the barney stick found close by.

It was now obvious that Elizabeth Raven was not going to reproduce. Jack's attentions faded along with his use for her. To make sure that no one else would have her, Jack had Elizabeth followed whenever she left Raven's Court. He kept her as a virtual recluse. When he got wind of his upcoming peerage, he found a doctor who was willing to accept the fee. He had Elizabeth sectioned at the York Borough Asylum, a mental institution on the edge of Naburn village.

Alice and Peter

Alice and her twin were illegitimate. Their father hadn't returned from the Boer War to give the girls his name. He died at Mafeking and whilst their mother's parents had rejected their daughter for her perceived indecency, the twins' paternal grandparents and aunts behaved as their father would have expected and raised his daughters with pride.

In 1914, the year before Jack had put Elizabeth in the asylum, Alice became secretary to the soon-to-be Lord Raven. Her twin sister took on the role of governess to the children of a wealthy family from Leicester, whose money was made in exporting coal to Europe.

Jack had high expectations of his brother and so far, it was all going to plan. Peter Raven was blessed with both beauty and brains. The thick traveller brogue that he and Jack had arrived with in the North was ironed out courtesy of the education that he received at Ampleforth.

Financed by the proceeds of Jack's blackmail and subtle extortion, Peter now had a soft and educated lilt. However, it became apparent that Peter had expectations of his own. He refused to marry the well-to-do woman that Jack had lined up for him. After managing to keep it quiet for two years, Jack found out about his personal secretary and his brother.

Well referenced or not, in Jack's opinion, Alice was 'not the right breed' and 'too old'. Despite what Jack Raven wanted for him, Alice had pleaded with Peter not to go to war, not to risk what they had together and all that they had planned for their future.

Taking her face in his hands, Peter rested his lips on her soft mouth. Where once he had felt her meeting his warm kiss until they were absorbed, enveloped one with the other, now her lips were cold and lifeless, as if he were kissing a cold bronze statue. His spirit went no further. He allowed his hands to fall heavily to his side. He had said all that he could to try and make sense of his imminent departure. He put his hands on her shoulders, trying to reassure her.

"We will be together soon Alice."

"If only we knew when 'soon' would be."

"It's now my Alice, here and now."

Alice tried once more to ask why and to order him not to go, not to risk everything, but the words would not leave her mouth. In her heart she knew why he had to go. They needed this last commission to be able to release them from the fetters of his brother's reputation and leave

Raven's Court behind for good. She knew that without the endorsements that would accompany Peter's return, they would be unable to fulfil their plans. He was giving up everything for her.

Without speaking further, he walked past her. Alice raised her head and watched him walk away from his reflection in the large gilt mirror above the fireplace. She followed him into the small hallway where he enveloped her in his army issue greatcoat, held her tightly to himself and layered kisses over her head, smelling the rose oil in her hair. Alice held his face in her hands, and she returned the warmth and passion that he gave to her. She could not let him leave without taking her love with him and offered up a silent prayer for his safe return when she would be waiting for him.

Peter left Raven's Cottage, set out along the track through the fields to the main road and headed for the train to London. His sweetheart remained sat in a crumpled heap by the door, weeping for the man she felt sure she would never see again. Not long after this, Peter left for a commission in France.

Jack tried his hardest to keep his baby brother safe and away from the warring, but Peter had secretly signed up to the motor mobile infantry. With a sidecar-mounted gun, they carried documents for the government and were definitely in the thick of the action.

This particular morning, after reading a letter from Peter explaining his actions, Jack moaned at Bobby in the study.

"Because he showed no interest in the woman's assets, fiscal or otherwise Bobby, I feared he must be a ruddy rump scuttle. I can't believe that they managed to keep me in the dark for two years.

"After all I've done for that bugger, for all of you. My bloody pain in the arse nutcase wife knew about it, about everything, and gave her bloody blessing, can you believe it Bobby? If she weren't already dead behind the eyes. Keeping it from me all that time. Where's the bloody gratitude, eh?"

Bobby was one of Jack's younger cousins. He had been employed to 'keep his ear to the ground' and so, unsurprisingly, he was fully aware of Peter's intentions. He understood Peter's motives but was not going to say so to Jack. As soon as everything was in order, he knew that he too would soon be leaving Raven's Court. Another cousin worked on the Sledmere House estate.

His cousin was now a Wolds Waggoner and Bobby was set to join him. They were instantly sent to the Front. Bobby and his cousin had little military training before they were sent to France. Their qualification was a lifetime of working with horses and the vehicles they pulled. Bobby and his cousin were not fighters. Their task as Wolds Waggoners was to drive along the Front collecting the wounded and body parts that might identify the soldiers who had died in pieces.

The early spring of 1916 saw the beautiful Jekyll flower gardens of Raven's Court turned over to grow foodstuffs, and a great number of sons, brothers and husbands from

the surrounding villages became fodder for the Somme.

CHAPTER TWO

July 1918

By July 1918, Peter was somewhere in Europe. Jack mostly stayed in London under the pretext of political business. He spent his time gambling and preying upon those with secrets to keep and chose to ignore the deteriorating estate that he had once been so proud of.

Alice walked into York, taking the tram to Fulford village, and then walked onward to Naburn. Birds were singing in the sun on the twenty-minute stride from the tram terminus. The long driveway passed through the beautiful immaculate lawned landscape of the hospital grounds. As she approached the building, birdsong gave way to plaintive and desperate crying, screams of anger and roaring frustration, gentle imaginings, and the placid acceptance of the inmates. Alice and Frances McArthur, the maid-turned-housekeeper since Lady Raven had been sectioned, were Elizabeth's only visitors.

The attendants knew little of caring. This institution used electric shock, ice bath and waterboarding methods. It was a far cry from the Retreat, a Quaker organisation on the Tang Hall/Heslington border in York.

A male attendant unlocked the door to the women's ward and ushered Alice quickly through it. She looked for Elizabeth around the expansive ward that housed over thirty patients. A woman approached and placed her hand in Alice's. The hand was freezing cold. Through the opaque skin, veins stood proud of the frail tendons that rested on the skeletal hand supporting them. She stroked Alice's hand, lifting it to her own cheek, singing softly as she led Alice to chairs in a bay window, where they were to sit together for their allotted hour.

"'Let me call you Sweetheart I'm in love with you.

Let me hear you whisper that you love me too.' He still sings to me Alice; every day."

"Hello Lady Elizabeth."

"Alice. How is Gert's garden? Is Bobby still clearing away the dead wood?"

Alice did not have the heart to tell Elizabeth that Bobby was shot dead whilst lifting the wounded into their wagon, or that the gardens she and Bobby had lovingly created under the guidance of Gertrude were now set with root and leaf vegetables. But Elizabeth Raven, nee Nice, already knew.

"They're blooming and beautiful Lady Elizabeth."

"Just like you, Alice."

Still holding the warm hand of her visitor, Elizabeth let her eyes drift out of the window and wander through the beautiful gardens that she had tended so carefully with Bobby.

When Jack passed through her mind, her face darkened, and her eyes sank deeper into their sockets. The light, which had just now beamed over Alice, faded into the recesses of her past happiness. The ice behind Elizabeth's eyes froze her tears. Alice kissed Elizabeth's head and

Elizabeth squeezed Alice's hand tightly in return.

Still staring out of the window, Elizabeth whispered, "Get out of there Alice."

"When he's back Lady Elizabeth, when he's back."

Elizabeth let Alice go then she drifted, back to the walled garden at Raven's Court, to sow Love-in-a-Mist with Bobby. Just in time, Alice caught the return tram to York.

Frances met Alice at the door. She had news that Peter had been shipped back to England in the June of that year. He had ridden over a land mine and been patched up in France but was broken in both mind and body. One of the lucky few? Just alive, he was being rehabilitated at a manor house in the North.

Frances slipped a note into Alice's coat pocket, waved smelling salts under her nose, and steered the faint Alice through to an ornately carved dark wood Tudor chair. Alice hadn't heard from Peter for some time. She had faithfully walked to the parish noticeboard every evening, joining the others who looked for news of their own loved ones fearing that they would be missing or dead. Although her heart had refused to think the worst, each step prepared her to join with the others who would end their days alone. Now she knew that she would not have to make those steps again and her prayers were for those at the noticeboard.

Urging Alice to quickly recover herself, Frances whispered a warning that Jack had returned from

London and was in the study with the doctor. They were discussing arrangements to escort Peter back from Howick Hall that coming Christmas. Alice recovered her composure quickly.

Once back in the privacy of Raven's Cottage, she took the note from her pocket and eagerly feasted on every word. Peter had not included the fact that the blast had deafened his right ear and that he was blinded in the right eye too. He would cross that trench when he reached it. Alice kissed Peter's last words: 'Until soon is now.' Now, could not come soon enough.

For one Austrian Document Runner, who's stint at the German Front finished early, the last months of the war to end all wars were spent in Military Hospitals, then from behind a desk. He ruminated on his own propaganda regarding the excuses given regarding the righteous German Army's defeat. He was there, alongside a well manned force, and they were advancing. He could not understand it.

1919

In the early summer of 1919, at the signing of The Treaty of Versailles, Germany was held responsible for the bloodbaths of The First World War. Breaking the French Russian alliance, after the assassination of Archduke Ferdinand was the only reason Germany stoved in. He viewed it as necessary. The Austrian, incensed by the blatant dismissal of the sacrifices made by him and his fellow infantry men, promised himself that he would return the world back to Germany.

Later, in the Autumn, Frances McArthur walked to the village noticeboard and pinned a sheet of paper to it:

'Lady Elizabeth Raven passed away today in Naburn Hospital, aged 42 years. Her Requiem Mass will be held in St George's Catholic Church, George Street, York, Friday 31st October 1919, 8:30 a.m.'

Frances blessed herself with the sign of the cross and walked slowly back to Raven's Court. She knew that everything was about to change, but that was all she knew.

The church clock struck the hour. Frances remembered that Alice would be on her way to give instruction about her things, so hurried her pace in order to be back in time to meet Alice. To cross paths with Jack in a drunken stupor was not a good idea but thankfully, he was nowhere to be seen when she returned. Her sigh of relief could be heard echoing around the empty deteriorating house as she went to the kitchen to make tea and wait.

Jack Raven locked the doors to the outside. He lifted a glowing coal from the fire and put it on the tatted rug that lay on the floor in front of the hearth. All too soon, the smell of singeing wool and wood smoke pervaded the air. He climbed into the garden through an open window, took a quarter bottle of whisky from his coat pocket, drank it, then threw the empty bottle behind him.

From under the ledge, he picked up two more bottles that were full of petrol and stuffed with rags at the necks. Then, holding both bottles by the base, Jack lit the rags, flung them into the house and brought the sash down. He watched the blue flame spread across the floor to the curtains, then strolled away to the edge of the woods, listening to the roof collapse between the thick stone walls of Raven's Cottage as it quickly burned to the ground.

Peter came home to Raven's Court in the October of 1919, a full fifteen months later than expected. He arrived in time for the funeral of his sister-in-law and sole ally. He was told that Alice, his secretly betrothed, had left her post at Raven's Court and had eloped with a soldier from the cavalry barracks in Fulford.

One beautiful 1920's spring morning, The Treaty, signed in the Hall of Mirrors within the Palace at Versailles, became implement. Now, Germany was being held to account financially, and the Empiric German territories were divided, some between neighbouring countries, while others remained under international supervision. The Austrian was introduced to Anton Drexler, head of The German Workers Socialist Party. From that moment, he understood the cause of Germany, if not the world's problems. The Austrian's ego, and the propaganda in his head, inflated out of proportion. The time to regain the Empires and cleanse the world of the deleterious had arrived. As if The League of Nations, gathered to ensure such murderous activity never rose again had not been formed, his influence seeped throughout society. His bitter scented, invisible deadly gas, spread once more across Europe. In England, Peter

Raven set out with Arthur McArthur to deliver a letter from a soldier named Joseph, who he had met before the Big Push. He had found that their lives were connected in many respects, but the main association was that of a tall surly man who went by the name of Harry Kennedy. Kennedy, they joked, was not of this world. Along with the letter, he was to present Joseph's Enfield automatic rifle and bandolier of ammunition, and a promise to the mother of Joseph's son.

In the summer of that year, now broken in heart as well as mind and body, Peter kept that promise and he married Margaret Bloxburn, Jack's original choice of débutante, and fathered a son. Shortly after this, Jack rested his head on the end of the barrels of his shotgun and Peter inherited the estate along with its problems. The footnote in the papers read: 'Jack Raven, brother of war hero Peter Raven, was found early this morning in the woods close to Raven's Court laying in a pool of his own blood. Police are not looking for anyone else in connection with the incident. Suicide.'

By the beginning of the autumn of 1922, Peter became a single parent widower when his wife died from influenza. It was a busy year.

CHAPTER THREE

1941

The world was once more at war. The remaining Raven heir was joined by those in the village that were not old enough to die the first time around. The Colebrookdale cast ironworks on the estate were melted down to support the war effort, never to be replaced. Raven's Court was left to deteriorate.

In order not to leave those closest to him in destitution, the tiny cottages on the estate were gifted to the McArthurs in their entirety. This had been preferable to gradually feeding what was left of the estate to the bank, the church and the government. The sole caveat to the gift was that the present occupants could remain until they were 'carried out in a box', whether they could pay the peppercorn rent or not.

In 1950, Arthur's son won the football pools.

Two years later, Peter Raven died, leaving no heirs and piles of debt. In order to buy the crumbling house along with some of the land on the estate, Granddad Arty gathered his savings and sold his furniture. He was granted a large mortgage of one thousand pounds to make up the princely sum of five thousand pounds which they needed to become the new owners of Raven's Court. The chapel and the site it stood on returned to the church and the missing railings were replaced by trees, dry stone walls, fencing and hedging.

Miriam and Little Arthur were born soon after the McArthurs moved into the main house. Great Grandad Arty's handiwork, joinery, carvings and sculpture, were all around the little estate, hidden in plain sight amid the garden, which was beginning to swell with the scents and riotous colours of an English garden once again. He carved a sign and attached it to the gatepost at the entrance to the drive. It read: 'Welcome to Heaven'.

The McArthurs arrival repaired, decorated and insulated Raven's Court. They brought the noise and joyfully rambunctious behaviour that the house needed to exorcise its dark and desperate beginnings. A new era for the house had begun.

Banbury Oxon, 1960s

The longcase clock struck twelve. Miss Edmonds opened the door to greet her visitors and they walked down the cool dark hallway. Her friend's youngest daughter was playing steppingstones on the patterned floor, tiptoeing carefully over the coloured terracotta tiles that led to the parlour. All the time, the little girl talked with people who only she could see. The child informed Miss Edmonds that they were standing in a line by the longcase clock in the hall. There were three short ladies wearing big dresses that made their heads look small. Alongside them was a man wearing a red coat with bright buttons on it.

"That's very interesting Little One!" Grace shook her

head before going into the kitchen and put some water to boil. Miss Edmonds placed the child on a Victorian daybed with a wooden Noah's Ark set that had been made for her father. She and her sister had played with it when they were children too. Latterly, as a governess, the set had been useful when educating and mothering the broods of children that were born of women with excess money and little inclination to care.

By the time Grace returned with pots of tea and coffee, the little girl's chatter had ceased. The child dozed while the two friends smoked Player's cigarettes and talked about family. Miss Edmonds lit another cigarette with her brass trench lighter, blowing an arrow of smoke from the bow of her mouth before telling her story.

"My sister went missing in 1919. They said that she had eloped with a soldier from the cavalry barracks on the outskirts of the city of York. She disappeared without trace. The last I heard from her was a letter confirming that she would be catching a train to Leicester so that she could stay with me until the execution of our aunt's will. Me and my sister were left this house. My sister was to live here with her fiancé, but she never arrived. Her fiancé came looking for her.

"Initially, he didn't believe me when I said that I didn't know where she was. The police were of little use once they'd dredged the rivers. They called me to York to identify a woman that they had pulled from where the River Ouse meets the Foss at the blue bridge. Thank God it wasn't my sister. Poor soul. I often wonder if anyone ever came to identify that poor woman's body.

My sister took just what she had needed: her savings from the bank, her important papers and a few clothes. To all intents and purposes, it looked as though she had eloped. She was seen buying train tickets two days before she was due to arrive here. That's where the trail stops. I miss her Grace. I have never stopped looking."

Grace held a cigarette to her mouth and Miss Edmonds held hers, index finger extended mid-flick over the ash tray. They both turned to look at the child as she spoke out through her slumber.

"She knows!"

"It's getting worse you know!"

"You mean it's happening more often Grace?"

"Yes. I reckon it started after the pond. Things go missing and turn up in the strangest of places, and every now and then books fall from the shelf of their own accord! Changing the subject, did you read that they have closed the case of the missing O'Sullivan child from the North?"

Meanwhile in Yorkshire

Vincent O'Sullivan was finalising arrangements for his sister-in-law to move to Ireland with her daughter Frankie. Time had forgotten that an O'Sullivan had joined the British Army in the last years of the 19th century, and the distant relatives in Clontarf, a backwater south of Dublin, welcomed Frankie and her mother home. There, he knew they would be safe. Vincent was not taking any chances since the sudden and suspicious death of his brother after the case had closed on the disappearance of his son. Suicide by poison and fire, or by any other means, in one of the cottages near the top of the hill above Ganche Lin was not his brother's style. He would die trying rather than give up.

Despite family protestation, the cadaver that was declared to be his brother was proved to be so with dubious dental records, fingerprints, and suspect blood tests. Even Vincent with his knowledge of the law could not find a path through it.

On the edges of it all, was Kennedy.

Arthur and Marthur McArthur

Arthur was travelling along with the circus of life when Marthur entered the world. Quite how he had lived and grown successful was a mystery to his family, but they didn't care. They were happy as long as he was legal and safe. He was a gentleman, tall, flame-haired and stylishly scruffy. He had the rare gift, that no matter where he landed, he was able to fit in with anyone he met. As yet he hadn't married, much to the dismay of his aunt.

Marthur's first galvanised memory of her 'little' Uncle Arthur was at the age of four. They met a month after she was born, then again two years later at her parent's wedding. Now, two years further on, they were preparing to meet him at the train station. It was a breezy sunny day. Marthur would always remember the excited squeeze from her mother's hand as the giant approached. She felt the butterflies travel from inside her mother down her arm and along her own, until they were fluttering around inside her too. Still squeezing Alice's hand, Miriam wrapped her other arm around the trunk of the tallest person that Marthur had ever seen. Marthur looked up but could not see beyond the jacket pocket of the giant in front of her. The wind caught her mother's skirt, causing it to entirely envelope Marthur in the swishing silk.

Hugs over, child unwrapped, Marthur was able to smooth herself down. She bent to pull up a sock and noticed his huge feet, like the roots of a tree. She recognised their potential for riding on. Marthur stepped back, allowing her eyes to climb up the trunk in front of her. They rested upon the dewy-eyed face of the man from the pictures on the walls all over Heaven. The sun was behind him and his big ears glowed red. But for the ears, he looked just like her mother, beautiful. Neither spoke. They just bathed each other in a smile, which had secured their bond forever.

Arthur bought property in the Lake District making England his base. He visited at least three times a year, always for Marthur's birthday and Christmas. In between appearances he would write to Marthur, telling her stories of his adventures, sending photographs, presents and postcards. Without fail and by return post, Marthur sent her drawings, photographs and presents accompanied by the reasons why she ought to be an adventurer like him instead of being at school.

A telegram arrived from Aunt Lizzie as he watched the

pink flamingos that waded, fed and flocked on a nature reserve on the Bangladesh coast. He was enjoying his favourite street breakfast of freshly caught bhetki that had been marinated in mustard and green chilli oil, wrapped, steamed and served in a banana leaf, all accompanied by a drinking lassi. The telegram informed him of the death of his sister Miriam and her husband in a pile up on the M62. Arthur left his breakfast to the dog under his chair and packed his passport, wallet, toothbrush and pager.

Twenty-four hours later, he arrived at the front door of Aunt Lizzie's Victorian York stone house in West Yorkshire. He was ready to take charge of his nine-year-old niece. Arthur drew a deep breath and tugged on the cast iron pull, which rang a doleful brass bell inside.

Arthur heard footsteps approaching the door. His Aunt Lizzie was a petite woman. She resembled a cottage loaf and always seemed to smell of cake and roses. Supporting herself with one hand on Marthur's head, she raised her tweed skirt with her other hand and lifted her leg to stride over the suitcase that lay neatly on the tiled floor. He listened as his aunt stretched to open the five security bolts on the door.

"Hello Aunty L."

"Little Arthur," she said, her eyes growing bigger as her 'little' nephew bent almost double to kiss and hug his aunt.

Unable to release himself from her embrace, he opened his eyes. There she was, waiting quietly with her duffel bag on the long hall bench. She was wearing a green coat and an oversized red beret with a pompom on it, smiling at him and looking every bit the image of her mother.

"You can put him down now Aunt Lizzie!"

"Got a good bladder 'as that 'n'. She's been sat there like that f'three hours 'as the lass."

Aunt Lizzie disappeared into the kitchen to make lunch whilst Marthur showed her uncle into the front room. White walled, hung with cuckoo clocks and other Black Forest carvings, the room smelled heavily of lavender and beeswax polish. It remained bright and sunny whatever the weather.

Arthur persuaded his namesake to shed her hat and coat for the time being. Aunt Lizzie reappeared with sandwiches and tea and placed these by the sugared almonds and bonbons on the occasional tables around the room.

"Aye lass, tha'll not feel the benefit."

Marthur spoke through a mouthful of Marmite, peanut butter and banana butty. "I've packed light Uncle Art, just my necessaries 'n' stuff. Jeans, jumpers, pens, a couple of books, my bear, bank book, passport and that picture of Mum and Dad's wedding. It's the one where I'm wearing a silly dress and because of the way you're holding me up Uncle Arthur, I look like I'm sitting on Aunty L's head, like one of her toilet roll covers! We're all on it so it had to come."

Arthur attempted to swallow a bite of his sandwich, but the lump of sadness in his throat wouldn't let it pass. He choked, forcing it on its way.

Marthur patted him on the back and exclaimed, "Take smaller mouthfuls and chew more! You'll be alright Uncle Arthur. I've never had a sister to lose, so I don't know what it's like when they go, but it must be very sad. You're getting on now. You've been left in my care. It's in Mum and Dad's will. I can cook so we won't starve. I can *parle un peu français* and multiply and stuff, so we'll be alright on our travels."

Before she cried again, Aunt Lizzie removed the plates and herself to the kitchen. Arthur wished that he could follow her.

Marthur wiped her sticky fingers on her jeans and patted Arthur's leg to reassure her uncle. "We're all we've got now."

Later that afternoon, Arthur and Marthur left West Yorkshire bound for Arthur's house in the Lake District.

It was dark when they arrived. Marthur was asleep, so with the help of Gloria, he put Marthur to bed. Then he sat in his favourite wingback chair with a bottle of Irish whisky for company. Arthur recalled his beloved sister, wept over her premature death and wondered what he was going to do. Children were fine when they could be returned to their boxes, but this marvellous toy was out of the box never to return.

The next morning, both awoke to find themselves in a whole new world. Marthur was familiar with her room at her uncle's house. It was where they stayed when holidaying or attending a weekend event, but they would usually return home after a two-week stay at the most. Marthur climbed up onto a bar stool at the work surface in the kitchen. She watched as Arthur made pancakes.

"Where's the first port of call Uncle Arthur?"

"We're going to see the headmistress of Mary of the Immaculate Conception Junior School." Marthur screwed up her face.

"There *there Marthur*," he said to her as he smoothed out the lines on her forehead. "Frowning gives you wrinkles and you're a little young for those. We're just going to introduce ourselves to Sister Joseph because you will be starting there after the holidays."

Marthur was not impressed. As for Arthur, England now contained the zest and excitement that he had searched the globe for all those years. A bittersweet discovery.

It was a full two months before the bodies of his sister and brother-in-law were released for burial. Arthur and his niece returned for the funeral. Marthur did well, as did most of the attendees that had never experienced the comforting channel of energy engendered by the 'bells and smells' of a full Requiem Mass before.

Arthur read the eulogy for the couple. Then Marthur stood on a box so that she could reach the wings of the eagle lectern and she read the poem written by her great granny when her mother had been born. "Many moons and skies ago…"

As she read the poem, those who were already in tears cried more. Those who had managed to hold it in thus far let out heavy sobs. Marthur finished the poem with a smile, walked calmly back to Arthur and quietly cried into the lining of his jacket.

Until she tripped over Arthur's feet, Marthur's attention was drawn by a huge crow, with a silver hoop around its ankle, hopping over the headstones, following them as they walked away from the graveside. Leaning on the wall by the gates, Harry Kennedy tipped his hat at the mourners as they left the cemetery. Arthur Mac Arthur bundled his niece into the limousine with Aunt Lizzie and Gloria and sent them ahead to Heaven. When everybody had gone, Harry stood away from the wall.

"Well now Arthur, it's been a long time."

"Not long enough."

"How long do you need?"

"As it takes to get rid of you."

"Nothing will stop me from having what's mine Arthur. Now The Druid's dead, The House want rid of you lot. You're all on your own these days. They were easy Arthur, like dominos at a rally."

Vincent O'Sullivan said goodbye to an attendee, just in time to stop Arthur from responding with his fists.

"As for you Vincent. Although I cannot raise your brother, when what is mine is returned, you shall have what is yours."

In the late 1970s, a delicate pale-skinned frock-coated birdlike man of law entered a house untouched by any notion of modern amenity. He found what he was looking for and his assistant searched through the piles of broadsheet newspapers for particular editions. They packed it up in a box as ordered and awaited further instruction.

As her feet grew along with her attitude, so did Marthur's dismay at not being allowed to follow her uncle around the world. Arthur managed to keep her through school, but university was another matter. Marthur appreciated that, school terms plus homework, divided by holidays, weekends and extra days off for saints' days, equalled a short prison sentence. Once discharged, she vowed that she would never enter an institution again. Her parents in the fleeting time that they had together, Terry her godfather, Arthur, Gloria, and now Maime and the nuns, had taught her all that she might ever need to know.

In the following three years, she became a traveller, managing to visit the places that she had read about in Arthur's letters. The difference was that now she was the one who was sending the letters and cards home, and it was Arthur who wanted to join her. In between her travels on visits back, Marthur worked in bars and hotels in the area. She enrolled onto art classes and attended auctions with Arthur, assimilating his art and antique dealing skills with ease.

One afternoon shortly after her twenty-fourth birthday, Arthur left a message with Gloria. It instructed Marthur to pack her toothbrush; they were going to Heaven. As they drove through Masham, Arthur sensed the burning question that welled up in his niece once more.

"So… why the sudden jump?"

"It's not sudden, you're twenty-four and it's time for you to take your share of Heaven. We're at Vincent's to sign on Thursday, remember?" Keeping his eyes on the road he added, "I'm building a shed."

"Nice. Are you going to live in it? Now that you can't run away, we can talk about finding you some female company. Someone not related to you in any way, who has a brain, is independent and doesn't try to convince me, you, or themselves that I'm 'a special gift to their heart'?"

"What's brought this on? One can't commit unless it's right. Your mum and dad were lucky to find each other. Young, maybe, but lucky."

"You're getting on a bit, that's all, and I wouldn't want to see you wither away on your own. Neither do I want to put up with wailing women simpering 'we must stay in touch' when they finally get the message that you thought you had made clear from the very start. Thankfully, they never do keep in touch, except maybe once or twice a year in order to find out if you're still safely single or wondering if I think that you may actually prefer men."

"Did you know that you're beginning to sound just like Aunty L? Has she been talking to you through your friend again? To put your mind at ease, I have been looking at new options."

Marthur showed interest. She had one or two suitable women in mind for him already. However, her interest was short lived.

"It's going to become an office. Maime went ahead yesterday to open up and meet up with Terry. He's looking forward to seeing you, it's been ages."

Marthur recognised the change of subject. She knew a full stop when she heard one and resolved to say no more on the matter of her uncle's marital status until the next time.

One and a half hours later, they were sitting around the kitchen island in Heaven, drinking tea with Terry and Maime. Greetings and catching up done, Arthur and Terry went into the garden to discuss the shed. Marthur stayed behind. She curled up on the leather Chesterfield sofa in the study with a blanket and a book, and soon fell asleep.

It was dark when she awoke. It wasn't late but it was getting chilly. She heard the crackle of the inglenook fire in the drawing room and with wood and ivory keys, Terry's chunky builder's fingers were gracefully freeing the angels from their grand piano prison. As always in Heaven, Marthur could smell her mother whenever she woke up. It made her feel as though they were all together, in the here and now, even though it had been such a long time since her parents' death.

Shivering herself from sleep, she briskly rubbed her arms and ran upstairs to shower and change. When done, she joined Terry who was trying to piece a jigsaw together. He was at a familiar table under the window in the dining room where a jigsaw of some description was always on the go. Terry handed a piece of sky to Marthur before he went to sit with Arthur.

"There you go."

"Thanks. Not a cloud on it!"

Marthur sat at Terry's place in front of the jigsaw. She studied the piece in her hand and attempted to match blue to blue whilst listening to the conversation around the table. Terry exclaimed appreciatively as Maime followed the aroma of the food she carried. Marthur directed her attention across the table.

"Hot pot! It must be important! What are you not telling me?" Arthur looked at her over Terry's bowed head but did not give his niece the answer that she was looking for.

"Plenty of time. Let's eat."

Marthur sat next to Maime. The reason behind the sudden trip gradually became clear as they tucked into the slow roasted hotpot. The Central Point had just come on the market. Terry and Arthur had been keeping an eye on it for some time.

Marthur knew The Central Point very well. Built in 1734, it was the mother of all theatres. It had been re-invented as a music hall variety theatre at the turn of the 1900s and was then known as The Gaiety. In its heyday, it had hosted the likes of Chevalier, Stan Laurel, and Lilly Langtry. With its own rep, it was known for performing abridged versions of the classics and served the needs of those whose entertainment was impeded by lack of both education and money.

Silent movies finally hushed The Gaiety's stage;

it became The Grand, carried forward by the likes of Keaton, Chaplin, Bela Lugosi, and Bernhardt. Pathé News, Bette Davies, Mr Bogart and others, chivvied and encouraged their audiences through the two world wars.

Notwithstanding, it soon found itself running to keep up with stereophonic technicolour. In the 1950s, The Gaiety fell afoul of the 1916 entertainment tax and closed. A short while later, it was bought for a pittance and renamed The Central Point.

The raked seating was ripped out and replaced by a sprung floor. For a few more years it hosted wrestling matches, dance bands and the mop-haired pop groups of the '50s and '60s. Sadly, it was no longer able to keep up with the advent of bigger organisations, rising costs and the growing home entertainment industry. The Central Point closed its doors, opening occasionally as a pop-up space for fringe theatre and the occasional rave, but leaving most of the once beautiful ornate gilded space to the dark, damp, dust and rats for years.

Terry mopped gravy from his plate and spoke to Marthur through a mouthful of bread. "The plum's ripe for the jam lass! We've got to get the pot on the flame sharpish because it's now open to offers, of which there are many."

The land on which the property stood belonged to various churches, as did much of the land in the city. Eloquent proposals from coffee shops, a health spa, a supermarket chain and a small casino (under the pretext of a leisure complex) promised employment and revenue for the local area. However, both the city council and the council of churches agreed that the community-based tender by Arthur McArthur and Terry Ashton should proceed. Arthur and Terry toasted their announcement, the crystal goblets ringing a clear B.

"We have bought the buildings and part lease-own the land it sits on for three hundred and fifty years." Arthur refilled everyone's glass and Terry piped in.

"We're splitting it as follows. Me and your Uncle Art, thirty percent, Maime and Cynthia Titas, ten percent."

"Are you sure that Cyn is a good move Uncle Arthur? She keeps trying to 'bond' with me, a bad sign! Besides the fact that I'm a little old for that kind of thing, I think she will take it as an invitation to romance. Anyway, who's the other twenty percent?" Marthur helped Maime clear the table.

"You!" said Maime as they set off to the kitchen. They returned with the chocolate mousse, the last of the raspberries from the garden and a bowl of cream.

The next morning, Arthur finished measuring a piece of three-by-two and introduced his niece to the shed.

"What do you think?"

Marthur considered the concrete footings and stud framework of the 'small' shed. It was more like a shooting lodge with decking. Boards from the old barn, which had been built by her great great grandfather, were strewn around ready to be useful once more.

"You really are building a shed. It's lovely!" Marthur

could not contain her sarcasm and set off to return to the house. Arthur brought her back, ushered her through the door frame and gave her a tour.

"This is a bedroom with a lantern roof so the night can come in." Marthur yawned and shoved her hands deeper into the pockets of her hoodie.

"Followed by the morning sun?" Undeterred, Arthur continued his tour.

"Over there is the kitchen and there's a small bathroom there." Walking her to another part of the shell, he traced a large square within the framework. "This is a picture window in your office area so that you can see your tree while you work, and the stove is going to be over there in the middle."

Marthur's tree was a thick gnarly yew, rent with age and almost as old as the abbey ruins themselves. It was often said, 'if you want to find Marthur, look for her in the Yew'.

Years earlier, Marthur had sought refuge there when trying to get out of putting manure on her grandfather's rhubarb patch. Her mother and grandmother were on their way to the tree to find her when a screaming red-faced Marthur had met them. She had been terrified by the rush of wings, big eyes and hooked beak of an equally terrified owl that had screamed close to her face. It was a full year before Marthur used the tree as a hiding place again and she always politely knocked before climbing in, just in case.

Arthur could see the cogs whirring in Marthur's head

behind her eyes as the reality slowly dawned on her face. Carrying a pile of salvaged Victorian floorboards over his shoulders, Terry approached them. He laughed at the scene before him.

"The penny's dropped then? I said last night that she hadn't taken it in and that you would need to introduce the idea gently."

Marthur tempered her words but was unable to control the volume. She responded a little too loudly for a sunny Saturday morning.

"My office. You didn't tell me that bit."

"You didn't drink that much last night Marthur. Have you forgotten already? It's our bag."

"It's not a bag I'd have chosen Uncle Arthur. Haven't you noticed that all my bags are small? Now suddenly I've been volunteered to carry this set of locked cases and I know nothing about the contents, nor do I know the combination for the lock to get into them!"

Arthur stood in the middle of the shed. He turned on the spot as he watched Marthur climb under the non-existent window frame. He laughed as she strode around the developing structure whilst flailing her arms around to express her tactlessness, her inabilities and lack of knowledge. Arthur took the boards from Terry and propped them along the only formed wall.

"Stop panicking! You've organised some surprisingly successful events. You've worked in bars, restaurants and galleries all over. You know stuff Marthur. You just need to put it all to your own benefit instead of lining someone else's pocket. The place is already staffed, up to a point. All we have to do is to draw on their knowledge and experience, do as we're told, and the rest will run itself. I reckon it'll be up and running in eighteen months. I've registered you onto some courses."

He took Marthur's cheeks in his hands and gently smoothed out the frown on her forehead with his fingers. "There there! Remember what I said about wrinkles. You'll be fine." Then he gave her a hearty pat on the back and returned to the building of the shed.

True to his word, Arthur kept on the longest standing members of staff, and they had risen to meet the opportunity to rescue the age-old meeting place. George looked after the front of house including the box office and he was happy to be left in peace to carry it. Gary moved from hot dogs, popcorn, canned beer and soft drinks and was promoted to café bar manager, while Ruth continued to book films and plan the programme of events. Betty dealt with personnel, keeping everyone in order. Marthur grew more confident in the project and her abilities, sinking herself into her twenty percent share of this piece of her future.

After two years of jumping through local government hoops, CP II opened its doors. It was soon bustling with craft fairs, exhibitions, workshops, studio theatre and live music.

The Lantern cinema flickered into life with live satellite performances and films to suit all tastes. The café bar hummed and buzzed along with cabaret, acoustic music, comedy clubs, and victuals to tempt the temperate.

Three tough but successful years later, Cynthia, up to now a silent partner with Maime, decided that she needed a hobby, and that CP II would benefit from her expertise and flair. The meeting minute was passed. Later that week, Cynthia cuckolded her way onto Ruth's desk, coercing her onto a fold-up events table that had been set up in the corner of the already cluttered office. She put up a whiteboard that was soon covered with platitudinous motivational messages to help everyone get through the day.

"You just carry on Ruth, don't worry about me. Not here to take over but would y'mind not moving that particular chair please, darling? It's the perfect size for my handbag."

Cynthia updated Betty and Ruth's system, thoroughly confusing everyone. Ruth carried on with her jobs and magnanimously embraced Cynthia and her 'little ways'. She even managed to see through to the good points in Cynthia, realising that whilst she was strutting around with her clipboard, drinking wine and mingling with the 'beautiful people', she was actually bringing in the fat wallets.

Betty struggled to explain to Cynthia that the staff were there to wait on the public and not to run errands for shareholders. Thankfully, Cynthia was able to stay away from Betty most of the time, only appearing when Arthur came in to see everyone or at staff meetings when she was in need of some positive attention.

One morning, nearly three years into her 'temporary' stay, Cynthia simpered to those assembled that she was taking a well-earned fortnight break.

"I've sorted everything. I'm sure you don't need me telling, sorry Ruth, showing you what to do. We've worked so closely these last few months, hmm?"

Ruth could hardly contain her excitement at the thought of being Cynthia-free for two whole weeks. However, two weeks became three. The 'flow' that Ruth had gone with at the beginning became harder to wade through, never mind walk.

It was now half-term and it seemed as though every school in the area had converged upon CP II. It was part of the council's terms, but it was good for CP II and good for the community. It was always hectic, however, this particular autumn half-term was chaos. Cynthia had booked extra acts to widen the audience and had forgotten to mention that, once again, she had altered the system. Betty, after hacking into Cynthia's computer, finally began to figure out a path through it all. Between them, Betty and Ruth had skillfully managed the clash between the live show 'Puppetry of the Penis' and balloon modelling classes for seven-to-nine-year-olds. The burlesque and pole dancing classes had narrowly missed clashing with Sr Margaret Mary's Irish poetry and storytelling lessons.

Instead of returning in the blaze of glory that she had expected, Cynthia walked into the fallout of her miscommunications.

Ruth, Betty Cynthia and Arthur were discussing the half term debacle in an ante room next to the box office. Arthur, unexpectedly called away by Vincent while the nightmare week was in full swing sat firmly on the fence. He was not in the mood. Cynthia perched on the corner of his desk.

"Can't you sort it out between you Ruth?"

"I'm sorry Arthur, but we didn't book the extras, so I don't see why Betty's and my end of year bonus should take the rap for the expenses associated with wages and free tickets to compensate assorted nuns, horrified parents and disappointed attenders of the cancelled, cramped or late events." Cynthia slid off the table and stood beside Arthur.

"I'm afraid ladies, this is business. All the information was on my system long before I went away and I…"

"And you forgot to put your changes on CP II's system at the time. You didn't mention any of it in the meeting before you left, because you knew we would not give it the nod. We are not that kind of cabaret during the school onslaught."

They left Arthur cornered in the anteroom with Cynthia, who was courageously trying to play her shareholder trump card.

After reviewing the situation, Arthur had decided to get off the fence and remove a few splinters. He concluded quite simply that as Cynthia's new system had been followed to the letter, the person to take responsibility should be the one that booked the extra events without informing anyone of the changes. Cynthia's tantrum could be heard throughout the whole building.

"After all the work I've put in over these years. All wasted. You take the side of the employees! I have a ten percent share!"

Betty and Marthur continued flushing the pumps and stocking up the bar whilst listening intently to Cynthia's rantings and the slamming of the box office door. Betty looked at Marthur.

"Poor Arthur. Don't you have a twenty percent share?"

"Yes I do, but I've still got to get dirty."

Marthur headed to the foyer to mop the floors and clean the toilets, coming close to running over Cynthia with her mop bucket on wheels as she pursued Arthur back into the office. Cynthia's voice went up an octave.

"I've had enough now Arthur. It's been too long and there's no change in the situation. I am totally invisible to you."

"I don't know what you were expecting when you bought in, but we have known each other for years Cynth'. Have I ever sold you any other notion than hard work?"

"Don't make it worse Arthur, you know what I mean. I thought it would be different working together. It isn't and so I'm going. You have two months to buy my share." Cynthia slammed the door to the box office for one last time, rattling the glass in the ticket booth windows. The sound of her stiletto heels click-clicking over the chequered floor faded as she left the building. Traces of her heavy sweet perfume hung ghost-like in her wake. After Arthur had bought her share, he held onto the share until George, Ruth, Gary and Betty were able to buy in. Cynthia was never heard of again.

Two years later, on a cold November morning, CP II pushed its nose through the curtain to Christmas chaos.

The post landed on the door mat. Amidst the bills and letters was a postcard from Pete, her oldest friend, who had set off to 'travel Europe' three years earlier. However, the 'adventure' had begun and ended in Cornwall; surfing, climbing, living with druids, hippies and artisans of all kinds. 'Back home. See you in Heaven, Thursday 10th. Can't wait to see you, P. x.'

"That's today," said Marthur to the Black Forest bears, "Typical! No ETA."

Marthur peeled herself away from the flickering fire and packed her car with boxes of brochures and assorted Christmas paraphernalia before driving through the foggy morning to work.

Pete got out of a taxi and walked into a job.

CHAPTER FOUR

20th September. Later in the 20th Century.

Marthur locked the door to her office and handed the keys in at the box office. "Goodnight George, see you Monday."

George took the keys and held on to Marthur's right hand with his left. He looked at Marthur over his half-moon spectacles, studied her face and wagged a slender but perfectly manicured finger in Marthur's direction.

"Yes dear. I find that pile cream, drinking lots of water and taking lots of rest is best for bags under the eyes. You should try it over the weekend." He kissed and patted her hand, then brushed it away, slightly embarrassed at his public informality, and returned to the queue of people waiting for tickets.

The hands on the large clock hanging in the foyer over the staircase waved at her, pointing out that she should have been at home at least two hours ago. By this time, she should be watching rubbish on the television with her feet up.

Marthur headed for the door only to have her exit thwarted by two couples. They were late and hurrying to pick up their reserved tickets. They opened the door to the café bar drawing aromas of almond, coffee and vanilla into the foyer and under Marthur's nose as she picked up the files that she had dropped in her attempt to escape.

The smell pulled her up. Unable to resist, she headed to the bar, knowing full well that one cup could keep her awake all night. Marthur, surrounded by a mixture of those dragged to the performance by a cultured spouse and those desperate for 'a quick one' before experiencing the chosen event, waited by the 'GLASSES ONLY' notice on the wall in the bar.

Silence descended as George announced the last call before curtain-up over the P A system. The room started to clear. Gary, the deathly pale goth behind the bar, signalled to Marthur that her favourite table was now free and that he would bring her tray out to her. It was on the balcony over the river. The last stragglers downed what was left of their drinks and hurried to the auditorium before the doors were closed. Marthur made her way to her table and allowed the chair that invited her to take her weight. As she started to relax, she laid her head back on the window and felt the warmth of the sun radiating from the glass. She remembered the files. For a second or two she considered pulling one out that she had been avoiding for over a week but pushed that consideration back into her bag along with the file. She gave out a huge sigh of relief.

"Is that you done then Marty?"

Gary placed the coffee tray on the table and folded his arms. Marthur brought her eyes back from the river and rested them on Gary's face.

"Soon. What about you? How're you doing? I see your fan club's in tonight."

Gary was a sensitive creature. He spent a lot of time

and money on his personal art (himself) and took this very seriously. He shook his head and nodded toward a trio of women all dressed in pastel poly-viscose and silver sandals. They came in every week just to watch Gary. They were helplessly laughing at him, quite openly. Gary sighed heavily.

"I'm on till the very end!"

Marthur pointed as discreetly as she could to Gary's face. He hadn't realised that the tickle he was noticing on his cheek was caused by a false eye lash coming away from the corner of his right eye. It made its migration down his face and subsequently landed in Marthur's cup.

"I suppose eyelash glue isn't what it used to be."

Looking down at Marthur, Gary was slightly bemused by her pointing and comment. He unfolded one arm, slowly raised his hand to his cheek and gasped quietly when his fingers touched his lash-free eye. He picked the lash from Marthur's mug and sidestepped to the staffroom to re- stick.

Marthur slipped off her shoes, put her feet up on the chair opposite and sat back to gaze at the river. The autumn equinox was upon them, yet the sun was still just about warm enough to keep the customers outside as its rays danced, sparkled and reflected on the water. A crane fly landed on the balcony.

"Off you go," Marthur said to the insect, "Take the gold up to the moon." And in an instant, the crane fly was gone.

Marthur poured her coffee. The caffeine steam prepared

her for the gentle hit, which would give her the energy to head home. Suddenly, despite the plethora of people around her, she had the sense of a presence in the room. She stopped pouring mid-cup and turned around. She saw a face that she hadn't seen for some time and had not expected to see ever again. Yet there he was, standing where he was not supposed to be, at the wrong end of the bar. Marthur noticed that she was holding her breath as tightly as she was holding the coffee pot. It couldn't be him.

Allowing her body to breathe again, she put the pot on the table and slowly turned to take a second look, but the face had gone. Half relieved, half disappointed, Marthur filled her cup. She contemplated walking through the evening's joy finders, acoustic groovers and partygoers passing through the bar to follow the face that had woken such a memory. She decided against it, telling herself that her tired eyes were playing tricks on her.

Once again, she placed her feet back on the chair opposite and settled back to watch the river passing through. The sun had almost set, and the starlings had finished their murmuration. The reds, golds, pinks and paler hues of the evening sky gave way to a cloak of dark Prussian blue, leaving a flame-trimmed turquoise cummerbund glowing between the darkness and the horizon. In this space, gleaming Venus, waited to grant a wish.

When the interval crowd reappeared, Marthur realised that she had been nursing her coffee for over an hour.

They snorted and chortled whilst either praising or pulling the first half of the performance to pieces. They trailed onto the balcony while Gary hovered around bringing drinks and lighting the heaters on the decking. He then made his way back inside.

Right on cue, George called through the P A to the audience, announcing that for the last time that evening they should take their seats. Marthur gathered herself together but was met at the balcony door by Gary. He was carrying a pot of coffee, a small jug of cream and an Irish whisky on a tray. Gary shivered, his skinny frame protesting at the chill of the first cold night in months. His silver bangles jingled in accompaniment to his chattering teeth as he put the tray on Marthur's table.

"In or out Marthur? It's a bit raw out here." Marthur rubbed Gary's arms.

"Breathe into your elbow then rub it. What on earth are you going to do when winter comes? Good idea, thanks Gary. Here I am trying to get out before the last hoorah and now I feel obliged to muck in. Tickets for the late-night cabaret have sold well and people will pay on the door too. It will be busy. Or was it your plan to get me to stay in the first place?"

"Aren't you the paranoiac! I don't take the orders Mart, I give them. Anyway, Art is in later so we can rope him in if need be. He's seeing a man about some furniture or something."

"Makes a change from seeing a man about a dog, I suppose."

Groaning at Marthur's lame wit, Gary picked up the tray holding the empties, spun on the Cuban heels of his winklepicker boots and headed back indoors. He halted halfway to the bar when he remembered the note that had been written on the napkin. He reached Marthur just as she was pushing her arms through the sleeves of her jacket. Without saying a word, he brought the note smoothly from a pocket in his purple silk waistcoat and slipped the napkin into Marthur's hand. Spinning on the soles of his boots, Gary returned to the bar to slice lemons and entertain the pastel dressers simply by his corvid-like appearance.

Thinking the napkin was to soak up the spillage on the tray, Marthur shook it open and moved to wipe it but stopped. As the corner touched the liquid, turning sepia shades, she noticed that there was writing on the napkin. Thinking it to be one of Gary's witticisms, Marthur looked up towards the bar but as she read the note, it soon became apparent that he wasn't the author. The hurried writing made her question the earlier communication between her eyes and brain. The note read: 'I remember that you said you like Irish coffee, and this is the closest I could get.' Heart now in her mouth, Marthur scanned the bar for some sign of the note writer. Everyone, as far as she could make out, was either involved with themselves or each other and were clearly oblivious to her presence. From the bar, Gary waved to Marthur, mouthing, "You ok?"

Marthur in response gave a thumbs up. "Yes, just

tired." She picked up the whisky. The warm rich peaty liquid was tempting but she was very aware that the second half of the show would soon be over, and the café bar would be crammed with the awe-struck, along with those struck with boredom, all clamouring for a drink. Marthur carefully folded the napkin note and slipped it into a file in her bag. She caught up with Gary who was having a crafty joint at the fire exit.

"Did you take the orders for interval drinks Gary?"

"I don't take the orders Marty." Marthur tutted. "Not amused? Mary took the order, but she left after the interval rush. Ask her on Monday."

The walkie talkie behind the bar crackled. It was George informing all staff that it was five minutes to curtain down. Gary squished the roach of the joint on the concrete ramp.

"Would you like a taxi, just in case you have a stalker Marthur?"

"Not tonight, I'll be home in half an hour."

Marthur took the strain and pulled on the large brass cornucopia door handles, original to The Gaiety. The glass doors slowly closed behind her. Marthur left the building and set off home.

Despite the light from streetlamps, shop windows and passing cars, she could still see a star or two. As she neared home where the light pollution was less prevalent, she followed the ribbon of stars to Heaven.

The cast were taking a second curtain call as the writer of the note left the lighting gallery and ran down the stairs. He walked straight through the bar and onto the balcony. The tray was still on the table; coffee and whisky untouched, the napkin crumpled. His heart sank. He drank the whisky, picked up the crumpled napkin and walked back into the café bar to await his friend.

After ordering a couple of drinks, he sank himself into a leather sofa. He looked at the napkin. What had been so unclear? He could never have dreamed that he would ever see her again. But there she was. Of all the bars in all the world, she had to turn up there. Unless, of course, he had bought a drink for a complete stranger? No. He never forgot a face. Especially hers. Then again, she might have thought the note was from a weirdo and that was why she had left it on the table. He felt better at this thought, smoothed the napkin and turned it over. Quickly realising that this was not the napkin that carried his note, he shouted. "She took it!" and the café bar, now filling with people, fell silent as its patrons turned to find out who had taken what.

After realising that it was just a man waving a crumpled napkin in front of his face, they went back to the business of waiting for the late-night cabaret to open. The buzz began to rise again with anticipation for the acapella six-piece, No Sleep, followed by the guitar and bass duo, The Ruby Larks, with their music and stories of 'life, love, death and madness'. He looked up from the leather couch to see his companion walking through the door to the bar.

"Hi, Arthur. Good to see you again."

"You look like you've seen a ghost. Would you like a

fresh napkin?"

On arriving home, Marthur flung her bag in the tallboy in the hall and draped her leather jacket over the newel post at the foot of the stairs. She made cheese on toast and took it to her room where she sat on the floor, lit the fire and ate her supper. The flames danced as the wood crackled with the heat. After showering the week away, she dried her hair by the fire. Pulling on her baggy red flannelette pyjamas, she fell into bed. The evening had sparked a memory alright, and it would remain with her all night.

CHAPTER FIVE

Eighteen Months Earlier

Marthur pulled hard on the huge brass Green Man door knocker. Years of Verdigris had contributed to its character. The nose, however, glimmered from the years of rubbing by those familiar with the house and the McArthurs who lived there. The door closed with a bang and the knocker hit its base with a loud clap that echoed along the hall and up the staircase. Marthur kissed her fingertip, rubbed the Green Man's nose, then skipped down the steep terrace of steps on the granite hillside and sent wafts of the sweet-scented aromatic herbs that lined the way into the morning.

She looked at her wrist as she reached the gate; her watch wasn't there. Pete had made her leave it at home. Marthur hungrily anticipated Eggs Benedict for breakfast followed by a walk on the other side of the lake and knew that she was cutting it fine for the 9:30 crossing. She had been boring everyone at work with the prospect of this break away for a full three months. Making sure that her bag was zipped and buckled, she set out to run. It was her last day and she wanted to make the most of it.

As she rounded the bend and neared the crossing, Marthur eased her pace. She noticed the full car park by the quay and was relieved to see that there was no queue. The foot passengers had already boarded but the kiosk was still open. There was still time to make it if she was swift. Seeing that the road was clear, she stepped off the pavement. She had forgotten that the roads in the area were not as quiet these days and that cars travelled faster. A car zoomed around the corner, screeching to a halt within inches of Marthur's ankles. As she attempted to glare at the driver through the car's windscreen, all she could see was her own reflection and that of the sky behind. She settled for mouthing at the driver vigorously whilst making gestures with her middle finger that were not at all genteel.

The driver's horror at almost having killed someone segued into excitement. He soon recognised the woman as she raised her head, her eyes flashing as her full-lipped mouth formed a lexicon of words worthy of his last coach trip to Twickenham. It was SHE!

SHE who had inspired him to pick up his cobweb-shrouded interest in wood again. He had noticed her almost two weeks ago in the spinney and then kept seeing her all over the place. But on every occasion, he had been interrupted just at the moment when he had plucked up the courage to speak to her. Now here she was, thumping the bonnet of his car and swearing at him. He'd almost killed her. What an introduction!

As he was about to get out of his car to apologise, Marthur turned to run. He found himself rooted to his seat, simply watching events unfold. Marthur was jerked back by her bag, which had become snagged on the bumper badge.

Now upright and angry, Marthur untangled her bag from the bumper and, with as much dignity as she could muster, ran for the turnstile.

The offending driver turned his attention to the tin of wood stain that was now oozing over the carpet in the back of his car. The emergency stop had sent his shopping crashing off the back seat. He reached between the front seats to recover the seeping tin as it glugged liberally into the footwell. Righting the tin and replacing the lid, he wiped the excess over his cream linen pants. He continued his journey.

The sign hung across the turnstile now read 'CLOSED'. Marthur stomped her foot and growled in frustration as she watched the ferry pulling away. She drew a deep breath and studied the times of the next crossing and set off back to the house. Her frustration was allayed by the thought of a fried egg sandwich, a mug of tea, 'Pop Master' and the morning papers while waiting for the 12:30 crossing.

Halfway back to the house, Marthur became aware of a car slowing down behind her. The passenger window whirred open as the car drew alongside, halting a little way ahead of her. The driver of the car leaned out of the passenger window. As Marthur drew close, she recognised the car.

"Need a lift anywhere?" Marthur resolutely continued walking, refusing to turn her head. The driver followed.

"I can take you where you want to be. Nowhere is out of the way around here."

Marthur marched on. Not being one to give in easily, the driver slowly kerb-crawled after her whilst leaning across the passenger seat to continue his conversation.

"I feel kind of responsible for your missed ferry. I can drop you by the café on the other side."

By this time, Marthur had reached the gate at the foot of the steps to the house. She stopped, brought a bunch of keys from her bag and looked squarely at the driver of the car. He pulled up, switched off the engine and leaned out of the window. Marthur was not expecting that the face of her would-be assassin would meet her gaze quite so intently. Neither was she prepared for the flush of pink that rose from her breast and washed over her face.

Marthur walked through the gate that had been left open by the paper boy and resolutely repeated her refusal. In order to reinforce it, she slammed the bolt across with a little too much emphasis, breaking her index fingernail in the process. She climbed the steps. The driver of the car shouted through the window.

"Small world. We used to rent the cottage behind the White House from Maime Brightlight. Living there or a holiday?"

Ignoring the statement, Marthur shuffled through the contents of the postbox on the first terrace, pushed her velvet troubadour hat to the back of her head, then took the rest of the steps with speed and grace.

He watched her walk to the back of the house and made the first turn on the ignition. He looked over at the White House once more, remembering the cottage that he had rented for his mother before she died. Two months later he had received the keys along with the deeds for a property across the lake. He made the second turn of the key and sparked the engine.

Maime Brightlight was the daughter of Gloria, Arthur's secretary-cum-housekeeper, who when she was alive lived in the cottage behind the White House. Maime often stayed with Gloria whenever she was home on leave. She had once been matron-in-chief at the Princess Mary RAF Nursing Hospital, often facing acutely stressful situations. This had honed her great wit and Madonna-like patience. Some said this made her calculating, whilst others resourceful. Gloria often said that Arthur and Maime were so much alike that they could have been twins. This was not at all flattering to Maime, being a full five years younger.

Her time served, Maime was unable to keep still and continued to travel, nursing in the Middle East and playing wherever the fancy took her. That was until Gloria had slipped one particularly heavy winter, ending up legs akimbo in a snow drift. Luckily, she came away from it with only a broken ankle, but it raised the questions that she had been trying to avoid. For the first time, Maime had realised that although fitter than many of her contemporaries, at the age of eighty-two, Gloria was not the spring chicken that she had been when her husband had died, and she had assumed the role of Arthur's other mother. The dawning hit Gloria hard. Arthur had been trying to retire Gloria for some time, but it had not been easy. Gloria looked on Arthur and his niece as though they were her own and even though it had been her home for over twenty years, she was still too proud to live in the cottage gratis as Arthur had wished. Maime hung up her winged boots so that she could look after her mother whilst her ankle healed. Meanwhile, they would hatch a plan for Gloria's future.

It was not meant to be a prolonged stay but, very soon, Maime's feet stopped itching, her travelling boots gathered dust and they were swapped for a chatelaine. Maime took over her mother's job as Arthur's secretary looking after his properties and other affairs. She became both ally and mentor to Marthur. All the while, Gloria continued mothering them all. Marthur trusted Maime implicitly.

Fastening his seat belt, he looked back one last time and was surprised to see her walking around the other side of the house toward the steps. In that short space of time, Marthur had decided that if he had been a tenant of Maime's, he couldn't be that bad. The thought of the spinney by her lake full of marauding hikers was too much. She returned to accept the lift.

Marthur rested her hand on the gate as she reached the bottom of the steps, wondering if she was doing the right thing. The driver of the car leaned over as far as his seat belt would let him.

"The spinney will be full of happy trippers getting away from it all if you wait for the 12:30."

That was enough for Marthur. She walked through the

gate and got into the car, pushed the button to wind up the window but quickly wound it down again, wondering why the car smelled so much of wood stain and varnish. The driver smiled at Marthur.

"Where to?"

"The café by the quay on the other side, please. That'll be great."

Once in the car, Marthur wondered again about her decision. Slipping her hand into her jacket, she felt the point of her newly sharpened pencil. She was ready to stab him in the leg through his linen pants should he try anything. A friend from her school days had used one to stab a boy from another school in the leg. He had become a little too personal during a dimly lit slide-show lecture on Cavaliers and Roundheads at the Castle Museum in York. It had done the trick. The boy had got the message and the girls had been evicted from the room.

It was a crazy summer, the hottest on record. As they bowled along the empty narrow roads, Marthur found herself actually enjoying the journey. The anxiety of the last two chaotic years blew out through the open window. The construction of the riverside balcony had caused lots of headaches due to unexpected planning issues and escalating costs. This had coincided with an extremely busy time at CP II. She had scarcely had a day off.

The driver babbled on to his passenger about various places that she may be interested in. Marthur, for once, was watching the world at work. With her elbow on the door and supporting her head in her hand, Marthur contributed cursory 'mmm's and 'really's to the conversation. She chose not to save her guide the trouble of telling her all about an area that she already knew very well. Her thoughts flew out of the window to follow a grey heron swimming through the sky.

The driver quickly realised that he was being ignored as he finished speaking to Marthur. He was telling her that her walk would have been out of bounds anyway by virtue of the fact that the lake was being used as a location for a new film in which Queen Elizabeth would be appearing. It was about to be shot by the lake they were driving around. Marthur hadn't even flinched. Eventually, Marthur realised that she could no longer hear another voice.

"Sorry. I was lost over there." Marthur pointed in the vague direction of the long-gone heron.

"I said, I can smell rain. I don't know how long you'll get today."

Marthur looked at the sky and breathed in the overture of autumn. A pair of kites circled high over a heavily wooded hill, thick with larch and spruce.

"I'll be fine. It won't come till tomorrow."

"Mmm," he said, unconvinced.

It appeared that the ice was broken. They continued along the road talking easily, sharing their likes and dislikes, chatting about the lakes in the area and how many times they had each reached the top of the Old Man by Coniston Water. Marthur deftly parried any personal questions that she didn't wish to answer, and the driver found himself doing the same. Marthur looked at the watch that wasn't there and consciously rubbed her wrist. On looking at the clock on the dashboard, Marthur suddenly realised that they had been driving for over an hour. She had been enjoying the journey a little too much.

"Do you keep your clocks fast?"

"Only by five minutes. Why?"

Marthur slowly slipped her hand to her pocket to retrieve the pencil. She placed it on her knee with the sharpened point facing towards the driver.

"There's paper under the seat."

"What?" Marthur replied nervously.

"Paper. Under the seat, the pencil in your hand." Marthur's imagination was starting to work overtime.

She glanced at the driver and winced as he closed the driver's side window against the cool breeze.

"Are you ok? Would you like to stop?"

Struggling to keep the nerves from her voice, Marthur replied, "We've been on the road for longer than it normally takes. I thought I knew the area, but I haven't a clue where we are."

The journey was suddenly brought to a halt by the red flashing lights of a barrier-less level crossing. The surroundings looked familiar to her, but it had been a long time since she had been there.

CHAPTER SIX

Dark clouds were looming, the wind was picking up and it threatened rain. Marthur looked around. Trees, sheep, dry stone walls… and not much else. She was glad that the words screaming in her head of her stupidity for accepting a lift from a stranger were not appearing above her head in a cartoon thought cloud.

Stomach churning, she put one hand on the door lever so that she could make her escape to who knew where. The other hand gripped the pencil tighter, readying herself for flicking the seat belt while stabbing him in the leg. A train thundered past. The lights continued to flash. What should she do? Her brain was about to burst. His hair looked darker now, his skin slightly blue. His eyes grew wider, and his lips stretched thin. A goods train lumbered slowly past.

"I'm not surprised you don't know where we are. You will soon. We've driven through the Bloxburn Estate. It's been open for about five years now. I did tell you we were coming this way as you got into the car."

"I thought they were stupidly rich recluses. Are they going to develop the area? Did you say the lake is closed? Something to do with the Queen?"

"No, and not quite." The lights stopped flashing and they moved on.

"So how come the great unwashed are permitted to rampage through the rest of their land? Have they finally been successfully prosecuted for laying man traps and electric fences on public walkways and bridle paths?"

"Not all of them. Lord B died and in his will, he named a direct but unknown descendant. Apparently, the result of an illicit affair in the Swinging Sixties. He copped for the lot on the proviso that he carried on the Bloxburn name. It was contested by cousins of the estate family in Ganche Lin, a small village in Yorkshire, but they were thrown out of court. The main house is now a working museum and a wedding venue. The land is still tenant farmed and the cottages on the estate are low rent to encourage life back into the area."

Marthur now felt slightly foolish about the thoughts that had gone through her head just moments ago. She ignored the fact that had she not been so rude at the beginning of the journey, her anxiety would not have been so high. Rounding the bend, the driver pointed across her to the café at the water's edge. He smelled of the sun and sawn wood. He smelled delicious. Foolishness gave way to disappointment as he pulled over and stopped. Now she didn't want to get out of the car.

The driver's mobile phone sprang into life with a 'Highway to Hell' ringtone. An invitation to breakfast remained on the tip of Marthur's tongue. He looked at his phone, then at Marthur, heaved a sigh and answered the call. Marthur could hear a high-pitched scraping leaking out of the phone. The tone in his voice married with the look on his face told Marthur that he was not in the mood for the conversation. Marthur felt awkward listening in but it was a small car. There was nothing to do but to make her exit.

Marthur gathered her things preparing to leave the car when the driver put his hand on her arm. He raised his eyes to the roof and wiped away a smudge from the cream header.

"No, I'm busy right now Coco. You have the keys to the office. Yes. Yes. Yes! I've told you, I'm on the way to the post. I'm still as busy as I was when you called this morning. No, I don't need a hand. Bye."

Marthur watched her travelling companion involuntarily cringe as two crisp rasps scratched through the phone just before he ended the call. He looked at Marthur. The sun was out again. He did not want her to go.

"What were you going to say?"

"Just thanks. The sun will be right over the spinney when I get there I should think."

Marthur got out of the car, pulled her hat on and leaned through the open window to thank him again. The gathered folds of Marthur's velvet hat fell forward and brushed his face. He was smiling at her, and she wondered why her legs wouldn't move. The driver wished that she would lean in a couple of inches more so that he could meet her halfway but just as he was about to invite himself for breakfast, a traffic warden broke his gaze with a swift tapping on his window, ordering him to move and make way for the workmen who were about to patch up the road.

"It's been a pleasure." He pulled away under the reproachful stare of the waspish warden.

"Yes." Marthur headed to the café unaware of the looks she was attracting because of the inane grin that had appeared on her face.

The café was busy with people fortifying themselves for the walk ahead and those returning or waiting for the ferry. Marthur decided to skip breakfast.

It wasn't long before she reached the water's edge. At points, the water covered the toes of her boots until she decided that they had to come off. So with jeans rolled up, socks in her pockets and boots laced over her shoulders, she continued along the shoreline. She walked barefoot over the sand and pebbles, the icy crystal-clear water cutting over her feet and enlivening every molecule in her body. Exhilarating as it was, Marthur still couldn't wait to see the spinney. She left the lake and sat on a rock, waiting for the blood to flow back to her tingling toes. Her feet were soon dry, and her socks and boots went back on.

As Marthur approached the spinney, she could see that a bench had been placed in the split hawthorn that she had known for most of her life. It was positioned so that Marthur was prevented from draping herself on the trunk in her usual manner. It hadn't been there at the beginning of the holiday and Marthur wondered when the new chalets would be coming. Marthur wanted to make sure that the person who did the job knew what he was doing with her tree.

Wandering around the hawthorn and talking to it, Marthur inspected the bench snaking around the tree, and carved out of local larch. Marthur eventually lowered herself gingerly onto the figure of eight. It was strong, did not touch the tree and allowed room for growth. Letting the Eternity bench take her weight, she sat, draped and propped in her usual manner. Truth be told, she thought that it was an improvement as she ran the flat of her hand over the top of the hardwood and traced the line of the grain with her fingers. As she felt the underside of the seat with her hand, Marthur felt a lump. She was sure it would be bubble-gum like she was used to finding under the tables after school holiday workshops. Curious to know what it was, she crawled onto the floor and aimed the torch on her keyring at the underside of the seat. Carved in high relief were a borage flower and a bee, the beam from the torch picking out the detail. She knew that the borage flower – its petals open, stamens ripe and ready for the beautiful, delicately robust and diligent honey bee was a symbol of courage and strength, a fat, happy little emblem that was mirrored on the opposite side. Marthur was impressed. She set her watercolour pencils, brushes and water flask out on the bench beside her and made herself comfortable. She raised her pencil, hoping to capture the vista before her, but found her creative streak to be stymied by the sun casting shadows of the branches onto the pad on her knee. Marthur allowed her pencils to dance around the patches of light within the shadows.

By the time she had washed the colours over the paper, eaten her packed lunch and tried the other half of the seat, the sun was glistening over the lake where it broke through the clouds. A late damsel fly hovered in front of her nose. Marthur blew a kiss to the creature. "Give the Moon my love." Then it was gone. Darker clouds were gathering again. The wind blew leaves from the hawthorn, causing Marthur to shudder at the unexpected chill. A sudden gust forced her to chase after the loose pages taken from her pad. Marthur wrote on a piece of paper, put it in a coin bag and to a twig that grew from a knot in the trunk, she tied it with silk thread she pulled from her scarf.

Marthur gathered her belongings, grateful that there had only been a few passers-by to share her ownership of the spinney then she walked the direct route back to the ferry. Once aboard, she leaned on the safety barrier on the top deck. The dark clouds had blown away, revealing swathes of fuchsia and orange above the wispy cirrus clouds accessorizing the blue. Smooth calm water now reflected the sky.

The craft pulled slowly from the quay. She could soon see almost the full expanse of the water, with views of the tops of distant mountains and tips of the wooded hills floating eerily in the bank of lilac mist now growing, floating over the surface of the lake. Marthur was transfixed by a pair of swans elegantly slicing through the water. They followed the boat briefly and then headed for an island in the middle of the lake that remained out of bounds to the public.

Marthur was met by a note on the hall table when she walked through the door: *'Arthur picking you up tomorrow love. I'm going on holiday to my cousins in Wales. See you in a wk. Maime, x.'*

CHAPTER SEVEN

Once finished for the day, he decided to take a walk to the spinney to see if she was there. It was dusk so he knew she would be on the other side, probably home by now. Anyway, he needed some air. His phone rang. Reluctantly he answered it, annoyed that it had disturbed the thoughts in his head.

"Oh. It's you. Signed, sealed and delivered."

"Yes, maybe, but I'm no longer yours."

"You never were. Just be grateful that this was business only. I am."

The phone call ended, and he drifted once more into his reverie. He was at the part where SHE got into the car, and they were looking into each other's eyes. The phone rang again.

"Hi. Thank God for that. I thought it was someone else. Fancy a pint in The Angel? You can tell me what the locals are saying about the one staying in the cottage."

"Sorry and sorry, early start tomorrow and I haven't a clue who's where. Don't you know the manager's number? She's not there but she knows everything about everyone. Why don't you call round if you want to know more about her? You never used to need a go-between."

"The manager's number. Are you in Maime's bad books again? Anyway, it's not that simple, I nearly ran her over today. I think she knows I'm not a serial killer, yet she may think I'm a stalker if I go round uninvited at night."

"Nothing is ever simple for you. Are you out of the cauldron, er, I mean, contract? Marthur's in the White House, go and ask her."

"Yes. It was signed over today. It'll sting a bit, but better than being associated with that kind of business. Anyway, I wouldn't know Marthur if she was stood right in front of me."

"You were warned. I've watched her grow up and women like that never change, but you rarely see them coming. I did mention it to you. Your uncle isn't fond of her business practices."

"Yes, yes, and my aunt thinks she's lots of other things too. I know, but it's done now."

"Does that mean we'll be seeing more of you?"

"Afraid so."

"Where does it leave your uncle's retirement?"

"When the old owl eventually retires is up to him, not me. He says that he has something more pressing, so you never know."

"Did Vin mention the bench and table, or will that have to wait?"

"You can send me some pictures of the garden to give me some idea of the space they're going in and I'll see what I can do."

"You're a gent. Your mum would be proud, bless her! I'll take some pictures and send them on. Be good." The call ended and he eased himself into the Eames chair by the window, thinking about the events of the day.

She was standing outside the car, her head through the

car window. She drew in closer and he to her. SHE leaned in closer still. SHE was going to kiss him. He could feel her velvet hat as it fell past his cheek, her warm soft breath on his forehead. Her face in front of his, he closed his eyes and moved in to feel her softness on his mouth. Nudging his forehead with her nose, she avoided his kiss.

"You're teasing me."

He was about to invite himself for breakfast when she kissed him on his nose. It wasn't at all what he had expected. It felt like sandpaper. She began to speak but a construction worker at the roadside started a pneumatic drill next to the car. He was unable to hear what she was saying. Her velvet hat fell from her head and onto his face. It was heavier than he had expected but he brushed it away. Her nose was touching his...

As the shutters of sleep were lifted, he found himself looking into the green eyes of Miss Ecca, a semi-feral cat. She had taken a shine to the house a week after he had moved in. Now she walked around the place like she owned it. Miss Ecca was black with a white panel that stretched down her face and onto her chest. With the exceptions of when she was yawning, bored with her surroundings or exhausted from a day's hunting, her oversized ears usually pointed up to the heavens. The vibrissae on top of her head and her whiskers were so long, she had a look of an ancient Kung Fu master.

Miss Ecca laid diagonally across his chest and the vibrations from her purring resonated through his sternum. Her long black tail curled around his arm as she licked his nose again. He took her face in his hands as she stood up on his chest. She walked through them, over his head and onto the back of the chair, where she lay behind his head like an ill-fitting antimacassar. Miss Ecca started prodding him on the shoulders and head with her forepaws. She wanted the chair to herself. He knew what was coming. The cat had already delivered a push from one paw and as no attention was paid, she stretched a forepaw past his face, splaying her claws. Still no attention was paid, so she gave him two rapid light punches. Soon she would be trying to stand on his head, gripping with her claws, so he relinquished the chair and Miss Ecca curled up in the warm space he left behind.

He didn't know what time it was. The room was in darkness. Beyond the glass wall he could see the blue night awash with stars, the lake fathoms deep and crushingly cold, a mirror to the sky, the surface reflecting the radiance from the second full moon of the month. He felt he was fishing for it and wondered if he would ever see her again.

The next morning he woke to the sheet rain of a grey miserable day. After breakfast, he dressed for the weather and went to the spinney to check his handiwork. It was the first real downpour and he wanted to see how it was coping. By the time he had walked down the hill and around the lake, the rain had eased to a light drizzle.

As he approached the spinney, he noticed a bag attached to a tree. "Bloody messy tourists." He wiped the water from the seat and then untied the bag from the tree. It crumpled as he put it in his pocket, intending to throw it on the stove when he got back. He sat on his bench, resting against his tree in his spinney, looking across his lake towards his house in the wooded hillside.

Shoving his hand in his pocket, he felt the crumpled bag and found himself curious of its contents. He pulled the note from the bag. The paper was damp, but the writing remained legible. 'To whoever made this bench. Thank you. May the love and memories grown around it be strong, courageous, happy and true. From a happy tripper.' When he got back, he pinned the note to the wall in his workshop.

As Beth Rudd, and her brothers scattered soil over their father's coffin, it was clear that the circle was finally closed, the thin thread of family connection dissolved. Not long after Michael's death, Joss changed the locks on his house.

Beth was in her late twenties by the time she was on good terms with the smells, words, or unseen but describable images connected to the living person she stood next to. Although there had never been any control over their manifestations, or their exit, the knowledge gleaned from 'The Company' which kept her was at worst a little embarrassing, but never anything to be afraid of. However, after years of being her father's scapegoat, emotional punchbag, and towards the end of his days his Taxi, confessor, nurse, crutch and bolster, the time she had in her hands since his death, soon became occupied.

After collecting some boxes from her father's house, she returned the keys for her flat to the Estate Agents, then she drove to her new tenancy. Marthur Mac Arthur, was already waiting for her at Raven's Cottage.

"Congratulations Beth. You are the first person to live here since the fire in 1919. If you're going to feel anything, it will be here."

"Thanks a lot Mart. Not what I need to hear right now."

"Sorry Beth. Only joking. I think. The Gray Lady hasn't been seen since I was a kid. Need a hand unloading?"

Beth shook her head.

"Crow Shore's said that they won't be here for an hour or more with the things from my flat so really, I have no reason to leave my history in the car."

"Well, you know where I am if it all gets too much. There's a welcome by the coffee pot, I know how it soothes your guts, and your Mother is in the fridge."

As Marthur predicted, Raven's Cottage was interesting. The poem Antigonish could have been written just for Beth. Exposes which had very little to do with her, were disturbing her resting moments, effecting emotional sensations and affecting her mental capacity, and the little man who was not there did not go away.

CHAPTER EIGHT

12th October

Saturday morning, 7:30. Marthur's large mug of hot water steamed up a diamond on the leaded window on the landing from which she watched the comings and goings in the mature garden. The gardener was attacking the roses for the last time that year and the spring and summer coverage of wildflowers, herbs, jasmine and honeysuckle were dying back or had disappeared. The trees hailed the onset of winter, their branches veining the sky as their leaves flamed, faded and dropped to the ground. It was going to be another bright day by the time the mist had fully lifted.

A squirrel caught her eye. It ran from under the hawthorn hedge, across the grass and up the gnarly trunk of the yew. As it descended, she could see it had something in its mouth. The squirrel dug by the roots, deposited its booty and, after one last look around, disappeared back into the hawthorn.

Marthur leaned on the relief of the window. The folder under her arm creaked, reminding her to get back to the job that had been 'in hand' for two weeks. Her sigh lasted the full length of the stairs as she went to answer the telephone in the hall. Before the receiver had even reached her ear, she knew the voice was that of an anxious man.

"Maime? Look, I'm sorry for making you choose."

"Hang on. Is that Dan? It's Marthur. I thought you were away for the weekend with Maime?" The person on the other end of the line hung up.

Marthur went to the kitchen and filled the kettle with fresh water. The gardener lit a large chiminea by the shed. She watched the smoke as it drifted through the morning, teasing her, whispering to her to come outside.

She heard the sharp clicking of typing coming from the morning room. Pete was working on CP II's website. Marthur sat across from Pete and read the brief out loud.

"Clear skin, clean conscience. Your introduction to guilt-free cosmetics and the life of your dreams. Working smart, sharing with friends."

Without looking up, Pete asked Marthur to keep her voice down. Marthur apologised before continuing to mutter through the rest of the brief, ticking or crossing out various requirements.

"One: Reception… that can be in the east foyer. Champagne, canapés, cheese… continental meats? I thought it was a vegan company. Two: Demonstrations. Screens, covered tables, four treatment couches or chairs? We don't have that. We're a venue, not a private events organisation." Marthur's voice grew louder. "Running hot water!" Marthur looked up and found herself alone.

Pete had slipped off to the study when Marthur had started to raise her voice again. She found her ensconced in a Victorian ox-blood leather club chair and she pushed the piece of paper under Pete's nose.

"Do you know anything about this?" Pete responded by snappily pushing the paper back to Marthur.

"Hang on, I've just got to do this." Then with a flourish of her finger, she pressed send. "Right. Now ask me again."

Marthur handed the document to Pete, who promptly dropped marmalade from the cold toast that she was eating onto the middle of the page. She wiped it off with a crumpled tissue from her pyjama pocket. Without raising her head, she threw the tissue into the cold fireplace as she continued skimming over the brief.

"Oh, it's that… it's been on your desk for ages. If they're still waiting for confirmation, you'd better get on with it. It's supposed to be happening at Christmas and then another one for Valentine's Day. Don't know who they are though."

Marthur took the now sticky brief in her fingers. "Fantastic, that's just how I like it. A year ahead is plenty of time to pick the flowers out of the bullshit that they call beauty, health and well-being." Marthur tossed the paper over her shoulder. Pete coughed. "Er, put your glasses on and look again."

Marthur picked the paper up, found her glasses and looked again. Then she realised.

"Not a chance! Valentine's Day next year is ok but not December. We're awash with fairs, exhibitions and concerts."

Marthur muttered at Arthur despite the fact that he was not there. She would let him know that he would be telling C-bloody-W, Walker-Kennedy, Director, that the answer was a resounding 'NO!'. She marched off to the kitchen to make the coffee that she wished she had made before she read the brief.

With the water set to boil, Marthur looked out through the large picture window. The leaves were piled for mulching and the gardener had gone. The chiminea was still alight, still tempting her outside. It was too much. She had looked over one proposal and she had had enough already.

"Fire's still going. Sun's almost over the shed. Are you up for coffee outside Pete?"

"Yes. My brain is frying. I'll build a number whilst you brew." Pete ran up the stairs.

Marthur carried the coffee tray over to the shed and set it down on the table. She pondered over two identical rattan recliners and sat down on her favourite one. She stirred the coffee in the pot, pulled the folded document from under the tray and managed to peel the marmalade-laden pages apart without tearing them, then she tried to focus on the task ahead, but her brain would not take it in. It did not feel good.

Marthur crumpled the paper, took aim, and threw it at the fire. It missed. She eased herself back in the chair and looked down the garden and towards her tree. She longed to climb in and disappear like she used to do. Her mind drifted back to the haunting feeling that she had experienced in the café bar just two weeks ago. She could still fit inside her tree, albeit a tight fit, but it was damp and mucky, and that mattered these days.

Pete opened the French doors from the study and clopped over the terrace. Her white clogs echoed, falling silent when she reached the side of the house that was not yet kissed by the sun. She left dark footprints in the silver dew-sodden grass and deftly dodged spiders' webs. Pete was tall, almost six feet, slender and gamine, every inch a time-travelling muse for Chiparus. Wrapped up in her Great Aunt Nina's heavy silk-satin housecoat she made her way over the garden. Large peonies embroidered with silks in shades of pink graced a midnight blue background, and deep quilted cuffs of the palest blue concealed secret pockets. A light breeze lifted the hem of her gown revealing a buttermilk lining that shimmered in the sun as she sauntered across the grass.

Marthur smiled at her friend of many moons. They had found each other and themselves at a high walled gated convent school aged ten. It had been their first day and they had mutually witnessed their first nun at close quarters, not just behind a screen or gliding past. The small nun, thin and pinched, reigned over the class of twenty-one, ten-to eleven-year-olds, employing her thick Irish brogue to the full. Sr Bernard set their first piece of work, to write a prayer.

Belinda Fryson, a petite polished creature, was extracted reluctantly from the safety of her desk to stand next to the nun at the front of the class and read aloud her prayer to Jesus. Belinda had a pet rabbit that would follow her everywhere she went. It followed her to the gate every morning and would run to meet her on her return. The rabbit had suddenly and unexpectedly died that very morning as she was leaving for school. Belinda asked that Jesus would, "take him up to Heaven to be with God and with Granny Fryson, who had also died just three days earlier." Her prayer prompted a resounding amen from the class.

Belinda shrank a little as the nun put a heavy finger on her shoulder. Sr Bernard's eyes were glowering from her wimple, the nun's monobrow casting a shadow over her heavy cheekbones, her sallow skin taut over her angular face.

"Animals," they were informed, "do not have souls and therefore cannot go to heaven." The nun warmed to her theme and went on to castigate Belinda and the class for their erroneous thinking. "God has no time for animals. They are here to serve mankind and not the other way round. Only the chosen, the good or the baptised go to heaven."

Sr Bernard was proud to have done her job, instilling the fear of God into small girls. The whole class watched on as Belinda crumpled. She remained thoroughly miserable for a full month. In summary, Sr Bernard's message was 'behave or perish in the 'other place' for all eternity'. Sr Bernard's expurgation became ever more zealous the closer she got to her retirement.

Marthur and Pete were inseparable from that moment on and, as they were well on the way to the 'other place' anyway after reading Edgar Allen Poe and 'The Exorcist' during mass, they might as well do it properly. The friends ruled the world, or so the nuns let them believe. Both girls left school with little in the way of qualifications.

At the end of the very last day of school, Marthur and Pete loitered by the school gates. They knew that once through the austere ironwork, they would never have to go back in. They had spent eight years trying to escape and now they would take their time and relish their moment of release. They watched Sr Gerade gather height as she approached, and they shuffled to attention.

"Well, well," Sr Gerade boomed as she closed in, "You two usually leave a dust cloud behind you. You're the first through these gates at the end of the day, or any other opportunity come to think of it, legal or otherwise. Now look at you. Everyone else has gone. Is there anything you've forgotten?"

A warm wind lifted her long veil, giving her wings and exposing her brilliant white wimple. It never failed to draw a grin. The nun put a hand on the shoulder of each girl. They felt her warmth and love, her deep and thorough knowledge of them, and her unerring support. She had flatly refused to expel them even when they had been caught throwing bangers into cow pats just as Sr Bernard walked past during a field study.

"Before you girls go, I'd like you to reflect on the deep furrows ploughed by your feet in the parquet floor that leads to my door. One day, there may well be a blue plaque with your names on it. I'm sure your reputations will live on in the classrooms, common rooms and staff rooms of this school, if not the entire surrounding area, for many a year to come, though I will be grateful that letters from the Bloxburn Estate will cease to land on my desk. You are welcome to come back whenever you wish."

Sr Gerade kissed the girls in the middle of their foreheads and signed a cross with her thumb over the kisses. She whispered a prayer for God's grace to be with them always and then the nun floated away along the gravel path around the outside of the school building.

The girls were unnerved to see heavy silent tears fall down each other's cheeks and quickly realised why they had been loitering. With the exception of one or two of their fellow students, they were already nostalgic for the whole system, even the time Sr Bernard had locked them in a store cupboard for three hours for laughing. They had missed Sports Day and had been delighted. They had made the most of everything. Now they were feeling a new emotion, and both realised that they were a little afraid of the adventures that might lie ahead.

As Sr Gerade disappeared from view, a huge crow flew toward them, retracing her path. It flew over their heads and over the wall. Arm in arm, the girls walked through the gates of Mary of the Immaculate Conception Upper School and into the next stage of their lives.

Midmorning in the Garden of Heaven

Pete picked out the Zippo lighter from the black and gold lacquered box she had brought with her. She placed the box on a shelf under the table then pushed the plunger on the cafetière with one beautifully manicured finger. Despite the trials that they had endured, her hands remained elegant and were complimented by her cherry-red-coloured nails.

"A simple but satisfying pleasure, like popping snow berries." She jiffled herself back into the lounger, covered her shins with her pashmina, flicked the Zippo to life and lit the perfectly rolled tapered reefer she pulled from the secret pocket in her housecoat. Marthur poured the coffee. "I've had a wave from Coral Wennal. She was asking after you Marthur. Trying to get through to you for ages." "I'm sure she was and is. I keep refusing her requests. What number husband is she on now?"

Coral Wennal had arrived at their school in the fourth form and became Head Girl by the end of her first term. Her tongue was as stiff and sharp as her starched collars. Her huge superiority complex and disdain for those less blessed in the hormone department did not fit well with the girls.

"Divorced again and in a business friendship with benefits with a Mr V.O.B."

"In a what?"

"She's a beauty authority. The blurb says she's a major shareholder in a cosmetics company. Her profile picture is from when she was twenty-five, thin and gorgeous, but I cannot access the link to the business."

Marthur tutted. Marthur's appearance and laissez-faire approach to the rules, along with Pete's refusal to make the most of herself, did not sit well with Coral. It was largely Coral who had sent them down that furrow to Sr Gerade's door. They were not friends then and no matter how many years had passed, how sterile, mercenary and anonymous friends over the internet could be these days, Marthur knew that she did not wish to be any kind of friend now.

"Painted and brittle springs to mind. She must be still colouring her hair red then. I wonder what she wants from me?"

"Isn't it funny how you gingers have been pariahs forever, but people still try so hard to be your colour. I always wanted to be ginger."

"I wouldn't moan if I were you, miss, I'm so bloody lucky not to have a grey hair on my head. Wasn't it Coral that smashed her teeth whilst climbing over the wall to get out of cross country?"

Pete passed the joint to Marthur and picked up the coffee pot to refill the mugs, but it was empty. She looked thoughtful for a second before replying.

"Yes… at least it was quiet for a while." Marthur looked at her friend.

"What have you done about the chap from the library? He came looking for you at least three times while you were away."

Pete snorted. Marthur picked up a couple of pieces of wood. Pete, responded in her best plummy BBC English, asked Marthur to put another log on the fire whilst informing her that she would make breakfast and bring back more coffee before spontaneously breaking into a rendition of David Bowie's 'Oh You Pretty Things'. Marthur joined in as Pete collected the pots on the table. The harmony rang through the air, sending the crows shouting into the sky and setting the dog across the field barking as they reached the high bits. Pete returned to the house with the pots.

"There goes Sr Bernard, telling you to mime again. Sometimes you just have to say it."

Elsewhere, a car had parked up in an opening to a field at the top of the valley. It had been there for some time and the windows had steamed up. From a distance, it was obvious that the couple in the car were having a heated discussion. The woman was shouting as she got out of the car and all the time, she could be seen flailing her arms around, and then she would return to the passenger seat. Then the male occupant would follow a similar ritual. Then, for the sake of variation, they would both simultaneously get out and row over the top of the car.

"I can't believe you've done it again. What is your problem? Are you dying? Or bankrupt? You don't know how to say it, do you?"

"No, I'm ailing for nothing… except what I've been missing out on for years."

"Well you should've settled with one of your many followers. I'm sure they could've provided your immortality."

"I don't settle, I make choices, and I'm not interested

in immortality of any kind."

"I don't do riddles. Mind you, I feel like I've been living in one big riddle for the past nigh on twenty years. I daren't even consider how much time I've wasted when my calendar changes at the drop of your hat. You take advantage of my good nature. You drop everything and float off to the other side of the world or wherever the fancy takes you this time. The pattern forming on the rug seems to be pretty one-sided to me and it's always in your favour. Over the last two years there have only been three occasions when I've gone away. Even then I gave you plenty of notice before I booked. The only time you didn't have a crisis was when I went to Wales with my cousin, and that was a couple of years ago now. I don't know where I am these days."

The pair sat in silence for what seemed like an eternity.

Eventually, he switched the radio on and The Ruby Larks singing 'Crush' rang out. *"You're here, on the other side of the world to me. I can't touch you, no matter how I try to unfurl my fingers."*

He cleared a circle of condensation on the window. A relative played the CD a lot. She said The Ruby Larks 'always had the right words for the occasion'. Unbeknown to each other, the couple in the car were thinking the same thing. The Ruby Larks were half-way through. *"Do I be bold or keep my distance? Well, I guess the former's best left, coz the closer I get, I lose resistance. Oh, do I move out on this quest? A minefield has been set. If I go forth, I risk my neck."*

She took a quiet breath. "I've written my notice. I'm handing it in at the next board meeting." She had dropped a bombshell of her own, on his heart, which he managed to keep from detonating.

"Is there anyone at home?" She switched the radio off and looked at her companion. Her eye twitched and her nostrils flared. He registered that he may have said the wrong thing.

"Did you listen to a word I've just said?"

"Yes, and I agree."

"What with? That I should give notice to the board?"

"No. Not ever. I agree with you. Things, well, *I*, have been a bit odd lately, but we can't stay here. There's a blue flashing light pulling up behind us."

A police van approached and parked. An officer got out, walked up to the car, and asked him to get out and show his licence. After a few cursory questions, he recognised that the two were well within the bounds of propriety and went on his way.

"Call again. See if anyone is in. Use my phone but just hang up if anyone answers and we'll go somewhere else to talk. We have to sort it out today."

"If there's no answer, it doesn't mean your house is empty."

The police van slowly drove past again and the couple in the parked car decided to move on.

Over Pete's singing, Marthur could hear the phone ringing in the house. She chose to ignore it. Going back in would mean working honestly, whereas if she stayed where she was, she could pretend that she hadn't heard it. If it were important, it would ring in the shed. Smiling, she remembered that the key to the shed was in the house. The caller gave up.

The file was under the table. Thinking that she really should try harder, Marthur brought it out and put it on the top. Pete climbed onto the worktop in the kitchen and shouted "no eggs" through the window.

"Beans on toast?"

"No. I don't think he's seen 'Blazing Saddles'."

"Who?"

"John."

"John Library? You're a dark horse. I made a breakfast bun yesterday, there's loads left, unless of course Arthur's had it already."

Marthur walked to the log pile, filled a trolley that was close by, wheeled it to the porch at the back of the house and topped up the chiminea. Half an hour later, Pete reappeared carrying a tray of porridge, fruit, toasted breakfast bun smothered in butter, and more coffee. They shared breakfast, chewing over the past weeks, the autumn and winter programs already under way for the weeks ahead and beyond. Pete was suddenly convulsed in a sneeze.

"Bless you."

"Thanks. I've been waiting for that one since six o'clock this morning." Pete brought a bundle of tissues from her pocket and blew her nose into one, then threw it behind her toward the open chiminea. It hissed as it landed on the burning logs.

"Good shot. How's the crop going Pete?" "Really well. Should be ready by Christmas."

"Great. Pass the file, I'll use it to roll another. Thanks for breakfast."

Pete dutifully passed the file, picked up the napkin which fell from it and put it on the table. It was now late morning, and the sun was almost as high as it was going to get before it continued its journey to quicken life in another corner of the globe.

In the garden of Heaven, the sanctuary of Saturday was the only place the friends needed to be at that moment. The heady blue smoke from the reefer and loamy wafts from the mulching leaves blended well with the light, the smoke from the crackling fire, the twittering of birds and the cackling of the women. The sun shone through the branches of the tree that they were under. Its light softened Marthur's glowing face. Pete sneezed three more times, each sneeze bursting louder than the last.

"Bless you!"

Pete sneezed again and scrabbled around, frantically looking for her tissues. Marthur grinned at her friend's paroxysms, ran her pink tongue over the sticky strip of the cigarette paper, picked up her lighter and struck it to life. Pete picked up the napkin that she had put on the table earlier.

Holding the joint in her mouth, Marthur raised her head and looked in horror as Pete shook the folds out of the napkin, drew in a deep breath through her mouth and lifted the napkin to her face in order to evacuate her sinuses once more. Marthur leapt from her lounger with a scream, knocking the empty coffee pot over. She stretched out her arm to bring Pete's hands down from her face. Marthur was successful.

Marthur's expression closely resembled Edvard Munch's 'The Scream'. It made Pete laugh so hard that she started coughing and almost drowned in the mucus that she was attempting not to swallow. This set Marthur off. In between gasps, snorts, titters and guffaws, the story of the napkin note unfolded.

"You never told me that bit. It's not much to go on though. Have you asked Mary?"

"Yes, but she sees so many people. And anyway, Monday morning is an awful long way from Friday. She couldn't put a face to it."

"Well, it must be someone you've had a conversation with. Think back. Who have you ever told that you like Irish coffee? No... don't answer... face it, Marthur, it could have been from anyone. Good job you didn't drink it." Marthur stared straight through Pete.

"Come on... you'll be saying it was the Ambleside assassin next."

"We were not in Ambleside!"

"Of all the bars in all the world, he has to walk into yours." Marthur remained silent but her blue eyes sparkled. Pete leaned forward. "You do! You bloody well do! Was he wearing a mac and trilby?" Marthur scowled at her friend as she lit the not-so-perfectly rolled reefer.

"Sorry Marthur, but how can you be so sure?"

"I felt something, then I saw him and then Gary brought me the note."

"Then there he was, gone! If you were so sure, why didn't you hang around? There are plenty of places to view the place unobserved."

"Dunno."

"What did you say his name is?"

"Dunno."

"Meaning you've forgotten, or you never knew it."

"The latter."

"How can you sit in a car for over an hour and not find out who you were travelling with? What did you talk about?"

"There's more to life than 'what do you do for a living?' We talked about *loads* of things."

"Except what *either* of you were called, or where either of you were from? Oh, hang on, he knows you like Irish coffee!" Pete added sarcastically. "That's something. What *did* you find out about *him*?"

Marthur felt that she knew enough but was beginning to regret not asking or answering more of his questions. Marthur and Pete, cleared the mess that they had made and returned to the house. The phone rang again, but neither of them rushed to answer. Marthur put the pots in the Belfast sink then went upstairs to dress and Pete set the taps running into the claw-footed bath. Soon the opulent granite and quartz tiled bathroom and the first floor, were filled with the scents of the geranium and orange oils that she had dropped into the running water.

Meanwhile, instead of dressing, Marthur sat herself on a window seat on the landing. She had decided to paint yet another picture of her glorious yew tree from recollections of a sunny afternoon in October using her charcoal and watercolours. However, after a while, she realised that instead she had painted the spinney as it had been on her last day nearly two years ago. Her bottom was becoming numb, so she downed tools and stood up to stretch.

Feeling peckish, Marthur went downstairs, reaching the last step just as the phone rang. She picked it up on the third ring and was greeted by silence on the other end.

"Hello? Is it Dan again?"

"Hi, darling. Yes, I'm in… I mean, here, what can I do for you?"

"Uncle Arthur. Good afternoon. You called me! You can come back and get some work done. How are the guests? Have you put them in a hotel? Hang on, there's a taxi pulling up."

Marthur put the receiver on the table and opened the door to greet the visitor. It turned out to be Maime, falling headlong through the door she had been expecting to stick. Maime managed to retrieve her balance and quickly rushed past Marthur and through to her apartment. She was looking more than a little flustered. Marthur could hear the small voice of Arthur shouting to her, so she put the receiver to her ear.

"Yes, it was Maime. No, you can't. She's just ran to

the back of the house. Anyway, I thought she was away? There was a call from Dan this morning. He sounded strange. A bit desperate. Do you know what's going on? What do you want anyway?"

"Just to ask when you're going to The Moon tonight and also to ask what Pete's doing?"

"I'm not going. Not in the mood. Things to do, things to discuss with you, stuff that has to be sorted by Monday. Vincent knows I might not be there, so... if you're coming back tonight, you can give me half an hour and then join the merry throng. He's been your friend and associate for so long. Longer than I've been alive."

"You have to go Marthur. I mean, I'm not here."

"Yes. I've always known that you're not all there."

"One of us has to go darling. Anyway, you really deserve a night out. Take my card from the top drawer and have dinner. If you set off now, you could even buy yourself something to wear. Take Pete."

"Aren't you the generous one! Thanks for your kind consideration for my well-being but the answer is still the same, and anyway, Pete has a date. Vincent knows how unsociable I am, and he'll forgive me. Enjoy the rest of your weekend."

Marthur hung up and went into the drawing room to build the fire.

CHAPTER NINE

Saturday Evening

Marthur walked up the middle of the wide oak staircase and went into her room just as Pete emerged from the bathroom, a bundle of pink towels in a cloud of steam, a full two hours after she had gone in.

"Bath's free Marty. Clean and running. Off to lie down for five minutes."

Marthur came out of her room only to see the back of Maime disappearing into the bathroom, locking the door behind her. Marthur didn't have enough time to register her objection. She settled for massaging her back and shoulders with the power shower in Maime's apartment by way of compensation.

An hour passed. Marthur pushed the leather buttoned wingback chair closer to the York stone inglenook in the drawing room. She reached for a spill from the mantelpiece. They were kept in a felt and card holder that she had made for Arthur when she was seven. Marthur flicked her Zippo, lit the spill, set the taper to kindling and watched the draw from the chimney pull a funnel of white smoke through the nostril of a sleeping dragon. The flames licked around the logs; the dragon yawned. She shuffled into the chair to wait for 'Father Brown' on the television.

Soon after, Pete swept into the room sporting Prince

of Wales Check Oxford bags, and a black cashmere cardigan buttoned up to a boat neck, complementing her perfectly symmetrical collar bones. A silver marcasite bow brooch finished it off. She placed a red silk and cashmere pashmina on the dresser.

"I thought you were having a soak. Who's in the bathroom?"

"Maime got there before me. She fell into the house when Arthur called. She wasn't expecting to see me, that's for sure. Is she still singing?"

Pete slipped the lid off her lipstick, winding the holly-berry red bullet half an inch out of its casing; without looking in a mirror, she applied it perfectly to her cupid's bow lips whilst flattening her Eton crop behind one of her ears.

"Yes, she is. The sun's over the yard fence so I suppose she could've had a drop of the Irish."

"Yard arm."

"Only if you're on a boat."

"No, she's sober. You're looking rather fabulous Pete! Very Vogue! Is it for yourself, Library John, or the event?"

Just then the doorbell rang. Maime floated elegantly down the stairs dressed in a turquoise silk mandarin-collared trouser suit that Marthur and her uncle had bought for her on their last trip to Singapore. Nervously, she looked through the viewer to see who was on the other side of the door and was delighted to see a beautiful bouquet of flowers.

Marthur rummaged through the magazine rack for the

guide and slumped back into the chair. Maime swept in. The arrangement of gardenias, Orange Blossom, and Lily of the Valley were placed on the table in the middle of the room. She fluffed the cushions on the settee. Strands of her hair fell loose from its fetters as she moved Marthur in order to plump up the cushions behind her and she languidly brushed them away from her cheek.

"You remind me of Katherine Hepburn in the film Desk Set, when she realises that she has found the right man." The comment was ignored, Maime focused on Pete.

"You look good Pete. Are you on your way to The Moon?" Turning to Marthur, she rested a hand on her shoulder. "Shouldn't you be getting ready Marthur?"

"No. I'm fine as I am." Maime tugged at Marthur's sleeve.

"You can't be going like that, surely! It's going to be quite posh!"

"Going where like what?"

"Vincent's do! You have to go!"

Pete emptied the contents of her small Gladstone bag next to the flowers on the table. "She's mooning."

Marthur threw a withering look and a cushion at her stylish friend.

"You haven't said where you're going Pete." Pete walked to the mirror that hung over the fireplace to check her lipstick.

"King's Court are holding an installation of…" She contorted her lips and wiped the corners of her mouth with her little finger as she finished her sentence. "Mwaanray."

Marthur suddenly stood up. This did not go unnoticed. Maime spotted her whilst studiedly placing candles in the sconces around the room.

"It sounds lovely Marthur. Why don't you go too?" Marthur spluttered, suddenly interested.

"Since when? They kept that one secret. When did you get to hear? How long is it on for?"

Pete called for a taxi. She filled her almost useless envelope clutch bag with her card wallet, lipstick, keys and phone, then draped her soft black leather jacket around her shoulders. She swept the remnants from the table back into her Gladstone bag.

"I didn't know you were aware of them. It's their first exhibition. Kings Court gave in and consented."

"At this level, for sure. I bet the insurance is astronomical. They must've got a grant. I think I might join you."

"Insurance for what?"

"Man Ray! I'd like to pull off something like that for us."

"Oh yeah! The Museum of Modern Art, New York City, asked Kings Court to hold on to the works so that they can go around with a duster… M and Rae not Man Ray! Exhibiting string."

"Never heard of them. I think your taxi is here."

Pete slipped her hand through the wrist strap on her bag and left for her 'night of string' with Library John. Marthur lit the candles in the sconces and switched off the lights around the room. She put Pete's forgotten pashmina on the table.

The couple parked by the field, had now parted company. The man sat in the car by the river, going over what he had said to her. He couldn't work out why she had run from the car when they reached the city.

Sharing each other's lives for so many years, he had realised that she knew him better than he knew himself. He had told her about the jigsaw in his memory, pictures of scenes from stories of his life. If he ever had doubts about his choices, he would bring the picture to mind, and it had always reassured him. In reality, he had known for some time, but unsure, fearful of the outcome, he suppressed the feeling for years. He told her that many complications were putting much at stake but could not tell her what they were. Instead, he told her, he had decided that she was the last piece that would complete his picture. He loved her. That was the point when she had run off. What was wrong with that? What was wrong with her?

He waited for a while, then risked calling the landline again. This time it reached its mark.

The scents from the beautiful bouquet grew stronger as the room warmed up. Marthur pawed over the arrangement looking for a card. The house phone rang. Maime answered it in the hall. It soon became clear that it was not for Marthur, but she attempted to make sense of the conversation through the door anyway.

"No, not alone. One's out, the other's not moving."

Marthur strained to hear more but Maime lowered her voice. Marthur tiptoed to the phone in the other room so that she could listen in, but the call suddenly ended. She sprang back to her chair by the fire. Maime sat down on the brass and leather Liberty fire stool casually poking the fire with the barley twist cast iron poker.

"All ok Maime? I thought you were supposed to be away until Tuesday?"

"Well, you know what *thought* did."

"No, tell me."

"All's good… didn't quite turn out as intended, but… it's fine. You haven't been out for ages Marthur. It will do you good to get out."

"That's a shame. He looked full of it when he picked you up Thursday. Telling me it had been a year. Expensive do, buying flowers out of season like that. What's he trying to make up for? He sounded stressed when he called you this morning. I think he was expecting you to be here. Was that him on the phone just now?"

Maime ignored the questions and continued to stare at the fire. Marthur stared into the fire too and noticed that Maime was humming along with Doris Day, who frequently sang in her head if she needed to think things through. Marthur decided to use the opportunity to catch Maime off-guard and continued her interrogation into Maime's odd behaviour.

"Staring at the fire can send you mad y'know. You're single out of choice, aren't you? There're lots of people your age in just the same situation these days. You've had plenty of opportunity and, like Arthur, you're quite a catch." Maime looked directly at Marthur.

"I'm waiting for the right one."

"You even sound like Arthur." Maime's cheeks flushed with colour. She turned back to the fire but not in time to hide her blushes. "Your cheeks are pink, Maime! Are we a little too close… to the fire perhaps?"

Maime stood up, walked over to the sideboard, removed the pictures and damask runner from it, and placed the pictures on the table.

"Do you remember having this one taken Marthur?" It was a picture of Marthur and Pete, both wearing silk and both dripping wet. Marthur looked over at the picture mounted in a silver Arts and Crafts frame and smiled. It was a good memory. Marthur followed Maime to the other end of the long room. She picked up the photograph on the way then lay on the sofa like a cat preparing to play with a mouse. Aware that Marthur had followed her, Maime began to dust the mantle over the unlit fire using the runner that she had removed from the sideboard. She could feel Marthur's eyes piercing into her head and heart; it was something Marthur was particularly good at. Gloria had found it unnerving, but Maime found it cute and cosmic. At this moment, however, she was with her mother on the matter. Maime raised her eyes to the heavens and apologised to her mother for poo-pooing her warning about 'Marthur the fae'.

"Yes, I do remember… very well, in fact. It was the year that you broke off your engagement to that rigger.

I know Gloria wasn't too keen. She said that his nails were too manicured. Real men have men's hands and all that, yet he told Arthur his 'ardour' for you was strong. His ardour? Which medieval etiquette book did he get that one from? Arthur found him hilarious. You gave us loads of reasons why you said yes to him, but you never really said why you changed your mind. And now Dan… he holds no love for Arthur, that's for sure."

"Well now, after that, I would have thought you and your uncle would know why any man that may show the faintest interest in me would run for the hills within a month."

"What about that chap from the brewery… when we were opening? I know you were glad when we had a hand in showing him the door."

Maime wondered where Marthur was taking her. She felt uncomfortable under the scrutiny and tried to change the subject. "Maybe I am. Have you eaten?"

"No, not yet."

The house phone rang again, and like two children running for the last musical chair at a party, both headed to the phone on the table. Marthur won the race. She picked up the Bakelite stick phone and put the trumpet to her ear, all the time watching Maime, who had suddenly decided to wipe the broad shiny leaves of the castor oil plant in the hall. She spoke through the mouthpiece.

CHAPTER TEN

Love is Deaf as Well as Blind

"Hello, you're through to Heaven."

"Am I talking to St Peter?"

Marthur rolled her eyes and yawned. She'd heard that so many times before.

"No, I'm afraid she's out."

"Who?"

"Pete! Oh, never mind… Maime's here."

"Actually, I'm looking for Arthur. I spoke to him this afternoon… I'm sure he said to meet him at Heaven and drop off some sketches. Only I'm running late so I've got to go straight to The Moon."

"Ok. But as far as I'm aware, he's away… some emergency in the Lakes. You'd better try him on his mobile. Thanks. Bye."

Marthur put the cone on the rest before the caller could respond and set the phone back on the table next to the aspidistra.

"It's ok Maime, you can come out now. It was for Arthur, or so he said. Arthur usually lets people know when he's not going to be around. He's been acting as though he's not quite there. Maybe he's one piece short of a completed jigsaw. The Great Aunt L always thought he was odd. Do you think he's ailing for something?"

Maime went pink again. Her face did not respond

whilst it stared at the underside of the broadest leaf on the plant. She struggled to extricate herself from behind it, then thumped out to the kitchen, shouting as she slammed the door. "What's this family's obsession with bloody jigsaws?"

Marthur jiffled into the chair, watched the fire and thought aloud about Arthur.

"He has been behaving oddly, more so than usual, but that's just it. That's why it's so hard to tell." Maime returned with a tray of coffee and Irish whisky.

"What's so hard to tell?" She handed a mug to Marthur and seated herself again on the stool by the fire. "Here you go, get that down you. Pep you up a bit. Would you like a drop of the Creature?"

"Don't need it pepping thanks. Just the coffee is fine. Cheers. Arthur, he's odd most of the time so how do I know when anything is actually wrong with him?"

The fire had burned low. Maime reached for some wood. Marthur began to sing but was cut off before she could get to 'breakfast and coffee' when Maime gave her a look that silenced her.

"Tell me again, who are the flowers from Maime?"

"I can't tell you again because I never told you in the first place… I felt I needed a bit of cheering up."

"Mmm, I'm sure you did, but who sent the flowers? How do you find the 'right one'? Please don't say, 'you know when you know'. But what happens if you know, but you know you can never do anything about it?"

"Then you do stupid things and become a pain in the

backside with everyone you meet. Then you scupper the plans of the object of your feelings in the hope they never have a life, so that they can be just as miserable and confused as you." Maime poked the fire with force, sending flames whooshing up the chimney. Marthur could not remember having seen Maime so agitated. Something was definitely wrong with her.

"Yes, I get it. Cynthia, for one example, and then there was that other one who thought she could get to Arthur by trying to mother me and being sisterly to you. They were fine examples from 'How to waste your emotional strength: Run After a Man That Only Wants to be Your Friend'. Why am I asking *you* anyway?"

"And your point is?"

"I'm serious… you're as old as Art!"

"Absolutely, and moribund to boot."

"Whatever! You're both still single and haven't had a relationship that has lasted more than a year or two between you. At least we'll all be together when we die. One bachelor and two spinsters of the parish surrounded by cats and home assistance, and then there will be only one left… likely to be me… who will be found by the postman, half eaten by the cats. Doesn't that fill you with dread?"

"Good grief Marthur. How mawkish can you get?"

"I'm not."

"We don't have any cats. I've seen too many relationships turn bad because of desperate choices Marthur. I'm not the type of person who needs a man to look after me. Neither are you. You're independent and a host of other things that I'm not going to go on about because I won't be able to get past your big head. Have more faith in God, the universe and, of course, yourself Marthur. You will find that the right person is under your nose. Mum used to say, 'If the people in the world open their hearts, their eyes will open too'. The mistakes made by one or another, doing the wrong things with the wrong people and thus hindering the realisation of happier futures, will cease to happen. You never see the right one if you're looking at the wrong one every day. You never know Marthur, if you go to The Moon, you may well meet the right person, the one who's been following you around."

"God Maime, I was almost with you for a minute there. Nice try but I'm staying put, and I'd rather not know if someone's been following me about. It sounds a little creepy the way you put it. What if you have already met the person and you can't do anything about it? Do you forget it and move on, or just languish in the memory of what could have been?"

"Maudlin wallowing gives you wrinkles Marthur."

"There you go again, sounding like him." Maime forgot her own grumbles for a moment.

"Is he married? Who is he? Do we know him?"

"No, *I* don't even know him. I just… know him." Maime stood up.

"I don't do riddles Marthur." Maime went to her apartment. Marthur went to the kitchen to find a full fridge but nothing to eat, so she decided to order a takeaway from The Happy Star.

It was now dark and the man in the car was beginning to feel the cold. The probability of someone else answering was too high, so he tried to call the mobile number, but it went straight to answer service. He tried again four times before he realised that he was calling her with *her* phone, and she had left with his. He threw it onto the back seat, tapped the steering wheel and tried to formulate a plan. Then he looked in her contacts to find his number and was not flattered to see how he was listed. He called her again. It rang nine times before a deadpan voice from the automated messenger told him that the number he called was not available and told him to leave a message. He hung up and tried again, but this time the monotone voice told him the number was not available and cut the call.

CHAPTER ELEVEN

Come and Stroke Fanny

In the kitchen, Marthur texted Pete. She could hear Sibelius' 'Karelia Suite' ringing faintly in the hall. Climbing down from the stool, she set off to welcome her uncle with a squeeze before giving him the task of sorting out the W. Walker-Kennedy mess and to tell him of his missed call. Instead, she saw the back of Maime as she rummaged through the tallboy in the hall.

"I thought I just heard Arthur's phone."

"No. Probably another one."

"Another phone playing the 'Karelia Suite'? I don't think so! We're the only ones in the house."

"I was playing my radio. Just switched it off before you came through. Radio 3."

"They play jazz at this time of night."

Marthur went back to the kitchen to wait for her food, then realising that there would be too much for one, she returned to the hall to suggest that Maime could share her meal. Maime, head still deeply entrenched in the tallboy, jumped up when she heard Marthur and banged her head on the door as she spun round. She was holding her hands behind her back suspiciously whilst keeping her eyes firmly fixed on Marthur's.

"Are you ok Maime?"

"Fine, all fine, just looking for my phone. Nowhere to

be seen. How's your dinner?"

Marthur moved towards Maime with an offer to help, but Maime refused both food and assistance and shot off up the stairs. She froze mid-step on the landing as the doorbell rang. Marthur opened the door to greet Beth. She had a letter in her hand that was addressed to P.H.R. Raven's Court. It was handwritten in ink using beautiful italic script, and hand franked with a postmark dated October 1919.

Maime continued along the landing corridor and up into the attic that spanned the length of the building. Marthur placed the linen paper envelope between the jaws on one of the ornamental Black Forest bears.

Marthur rubbed the bears' heads and then went back into the kitchen to set a place on the island ready to eat. A message pinged through from Pete: 'How long is a piece of string? I now know all about the fascinating intricacies and quirks of library systems. YAWN! Didn't know what to expect but it definitely wasn't being wrapped up in coloured string that represented the tangles of life! I'm covered in bits of hemp, didn't get it. How's Father Brown?'

'Too busy. Maime's being very odd. She keeps trying to get me to go out and I know that it's not for my benefit. Waiting for a Happy Star special. Please call Maime, then Arthur. You have a letter.'

When the doorbell rang, Maime briefly stopped her rooting, stomping and rummaging in the attic. She started again when she smelled Marthur's dinner. Marthur was enjoying the challenge of eating her food with jade chopsticks whilst simultaneously doing the crossword in the weekend broadsheet. Pete pinged back: 'Straight to answer service, the other's unavailable. HELP! John has brought a friend. Please come out. They're going to The Moon too!' Marthur swapped to a fork.

As she finished the last fork-full of noodles on her plate, Pete pinged through again. She wiped away the remnants of ginger and spring onion sauce that had dribbled on to her chin. Marthur put the rest of the food on the marble shelf in the larder and opened the message. 'Taxi on its way to pick you up. See you soon. Thank you!'

Marthur had two choices. Number one, call all of Pete's usual taxi firms to cancel the taxi and then risk one arriving before she had time to change and have to pay for it anyway. Number two, bite the bullet, rescue Pete from her date with the Central Library's logging system and rescue herself from the twitching Maime.

Maime heard Marthur run upstairs and into her room. She waited in Arthur's bedroom until she was absolutely sure that Marthur was staying where she was, then crept down the stairs in the dark. She needed to make a call privately in her apartment.

Headlights shone through the windows like search beams as the car Maime heard travelling along the gravel driveway up to the house swung round the horseshoe.

She didn't recognise the engine and waited by the door.

Marthur heard it too. She walked from her room with her Crombie coat over her arm and flicked the switch for the lamp on the tuffet by her door. It gently illuminated the floor to the edge of the landing.

Marthur looked over the balustrade. Maime, standing on tiptoes, peered out through the spy eye in the door. Obviously unaware of anyone else, Maime jumped like a scalded cat when Marthur switched the lights on in the hall from the top of the stairs and the doorbell rang. By the time Marthur reached the quarter turn, Maime had hesitantly opened the door.

Burt looked over his shoulder as he walked back to the car. "Taxi for McArthur."

"*Really*?"

"That was a little too hearty Maime, anyone would think you wanted me out."

By this time, Maime was blushing all over her body and her breathing was quick, whether through nerves or from excitement, Marthur could not be sure. It could be the coffee she had drunk earlier but she hadn't had any Irish… as far as she was aware. Marthur didn't like the look of her at all.

"Listen, Maime, you look like you're running a bug or something. I know you haven't eaten. I'm going to stay in and look after you, wrap you up in a warm blanket. I'm sorry that I told Arthur that you were here. I hope that he hasn't given you a crisis to sort, or is that why you're back? Has he done it again and asked you to cut your holiday short?"

The taxi driver tooted twice. Marthur attempted to drape her coat over the newel post at the foot of the stairs and her arm around Maime, but Maime turned away from the comforting gesture, put the coat back over Marthur's arm and assisted her through the door, insisting that she was fine and more than happy to be alone.

Marthur slid onto the back seat of the car. The driver turned up the heater, wound down the rear passenger window and handed a joint to Marthur.

"Have it now if you like Marty. It's just a little thank you for what you did for Anthea's Fanny."

Anthea's Fanny was a Chinese pygmy pig that Burt and his wife had bought as a pet, but inevitably it had grown too big, so Marthur had taken her as a present for Arthur and she lived in the orchard at Heaven.

"Cheers Burt. I'll save it for later."

Burt wound the window back up and fifteen minutes later, they pulled up outside The Moon. It was one of the oldest family-run coaching inns in the country and had a history that included priest holes, plots and rebellions. Marthur got out of the car and handed the money to Burt. A motorbike roared by, and she had to shout her goodbye.

"You can come and stroke Anthea's Fanny whenever you like."

A couple walking past, stiff and old before their time, looked shocked and tutted loudly at Marthur's expressive offer and her short skirt. Burt could not resist shouting after them, "That's your dirty minds."

Marthur walked through the heavy 18th century oak

doors that were furnished with gleaming brass, the wood preserved under layers of black paint. She headed up a wide ornate staircase to the first floor and into The Sea of Tranquillity, which was anything but. As she approached the function room, the doors were opened by two doormen dressed in Georgian livery. Pete was waiting on the other side of the door. She linked her arm, span her round and escorted Marthur protesting up the second flight of stairs. She had wanted to say hello to Vincent.

Two more footmen opened the doors to the oak-panelled boardroom. Crystal chandeliers hung by chains from the ceiling, and sconces on the walls and tables gave a warm light that bounced off the large gilt mirrors hanging all around the room.

It was a place to be slow and easy, secreted away from the hubbub on the floor below. People from all over the country and far-flung corners of everywhere had come to wish Vincent well. The gentle murmurings and the rolling chatter were interspersed with shouts across the room to familiar faces last seen long ago. All was accompanied by subtle vintage soul grooves spun from the DJ's deck. They made their way to a table at the most dimly lit end of the room under the minstrels' gallery and Pete pressed a bell on the wall. Before they had removed their gloves, a waiter appeared to take their order for two absinthes. He disappeared through a panel in the wall and headed along a hidden passage that ensured that staff could move efficiently and were only seen when needed.

"You managed to escape from Library John and his

friend… I hope! I've come to rescue you, not double up."

"I thought I'd try someone normal for a change. He's lovely but I, who knew nothing of computer gaming or ever wants to for that matter, now know almost as much as the average library systems manager. The only thing of interest was the role players' outfits. Then his lupine friend loped over and stroked my bottom at Kings Court. I wasn't absolutely sure it was him until he gently pushed some hair behind a waitress's ear while she was offering us canapés."

The waiter returned with their drinks through the panelled wall. He set fire to some of the absinthe and brown sugar before adding it to the absinthe and water in the glasses. He then slipped away through another panel and was gone.

"I said goodbye halfway through the evening and told them that I was going to meet you. Then Mr Lupine waved his ticket and said, 'I've shown you mine!' They walked me here to defend me from the 'rogues of the night'. I did tell them in no uncertain terms that there was no need, and I haven't seen them since I got here."

"Lucky escape then. Have you seen Vincent?"

"Yes. He said he would like to see you at some point. He mentioned having a word with you. He's looking good for his age. I hope I look like that when I get there."

"With more hair on your chin than head?"

The space gradually filled with people. The music went up a notch in both volume and bass, sending ribbons of rhythm that wrapped around everyone in the room in preparation for the band that were yet to come. The vibrations from people walking across the floor travelled up the central column of the table that supported the elbows leaning on its surface. The tremors surging up the stems of the large brandy bowls pushed the refracted ricocheting reflection of the flame from the candle through the viscous contents of the glass. Ethereal shapes danced along to the throbbing music as flying wings of light bounced off the highly polished surface of the heavy circular oak table. Marthur raised her glass and the wings disappeared. They made a toast to the Green Fairy before white noise and shrieking feedback sounding through the speaker just above Marthur, made them both wince. Someone tapped the microphone twice and coughed, then the whole building roared in response when the voice asked if he could be heard. "It's great to see so many people from so far away still keeping their connection after so many years." The voice spoke on about various incidents in his uncle's history. It was a long speech. Eventually everyone was asked to raise their glasses and be upstanding to toast the health of Mr Vincent O'Sullivan.

The band took to the stage, laying down compelling fusions of jazz-funk, soul, and drum and bass which, much to the detriment of unaccustomed aching muscles the next morning, enticed people to dance late into the night. It was loud and bounced through every room in the building.

Pete noticed the empty glasses on the table and pulled

Marthur closer to her. Marthur put her finger in her ear in order to hear what Pete was trying to say.

"Press the bell? Dance or go outside?" Marthur thumbed towards the door.

"Outside! I've got Granny's case."

They left the building, crossed the road to Gallery Square and sat on one of the benches behind the fountain in front of the art gallery and the old art school.

CHAPTER TWELVE

The Street is a River

Marthur retrieved a silver cigarette case from her pocket, popped it open and offered it to Pete. She took out two reefers and handed one to Marthur. Leaning back on the bench, they folded their legs conspiratorially in each other's direction and lit the joints. Through the changing veil of colours from the gurgling twinkling fountain, they watched the comings and goings of The Moon.

Marthur took a small bag from another pocket and emptied it out onto Pete's lap as she shivered, wishing that she hadn't forgotten her pashmina wrap. Pete gratefully swathed the red pashmina around her head and shoulders. Marthur pointed to the fountain.

"Do you remember the tea party we had in there when we were eighteen and still ridiculous?"

"Certainly do. It was an extremely hot summer. Your silk taffeta dress was amazing until we had to cut you out of it when it shrank, and you couldn't breathe. Happy hazy days."

The town hall clock chimed the third quarter. "In for the last hour?"

Pete stood up, made sure nothing had stuck to her bottom, pulled Marthur to standing, then sat back down again and pointed to The Moon. John and his mate were hanging around the entrance. Marthur stood up, pulling

Pete with her.

"Stuff that. It's too cold."

The women walked arm in arm, stopping the traffic so that they could cross the road.

John took hold of Pete's elbow as they reached the cast iron railings, whose sole purpose was to stop the public falling into the cellar under The Moon.

"We've been looking for you for a while. We were just going, but… now you're here." John's friend sidled up to Marthur and stroked her arm with his finger.

"Hey. What have we got here? I'm Tony and I approve!"

Marthur allowed the stroking to continue, held Tony's gaze and leaned towards him, either to kiss his cheek or to wrap him in a warm embrace, Tony could not be sure. Either would be welcome, but she only answered his question.

"I don't know what you've got, but I like to get things open from the start. I'm Marthur. How do you do. I've got chlamydia, so I…"

Before she could finish her sentence, Tony was on the back foot and in his haste to get away, he scraped his sock-less ankle, scuffing his red patent loafers on the stone footings of the railings. Meanwhile, Marthur pointed to her groin and turned to Pete.

"Have you brought the wipes Daaahling? Feeling itchy. I need the ladies."

Tony removed his hand from his pocket and fumbled to button up his pale silver-blue jacket. After making excuses to John, he clomped rhythmlessly into the night, the shiny fabric of his suit reflecting the streetlights as he walked. Marthur and Pete waved him off from the door and John stepped up to follow them but got no further than the second step up. Pete put a hand on his shoulder and sent him off too. Then she followed Marthur to the cloak room.

Pete's voice echoed through the Victorian tiled cubicle of the ladies toilets.

"You do realise you told the whole square that you have chlamydia?"

"And do you realise that you have now told The Moon?"

"And the difference is?"

"The street is like a river. Words pass through the air and are diluted by other sounds until the air takes them. We are in an echo chamber, and the echo is passed on by other bodies and the dissipation is not so quick."

A toilet flushed. The women fell silent until whomever it was had left the ladies. Marthur and Pete came out of the cubicles, peering at their reflections in the foxed and flaking mirrors while simultaneously washing their hands and applying lipstick.

Arm in arm, they swung through the double doors and took themselves off to The Sea of Tranquillity to find Vincent before the band started their second set.

The liveried footmen opened the doors as they approached and the two swam through the suits and dresses of the multitude there. All present carried stories of Vincent's life, a champion of many and a respected opponent of others. He knew the law and used its foibles to his advantage and for those who were lucky enough to engage his skills.

Tripping, dancing and weaving through the bodies, Pete managed to reach the bar. Meanwhile, Marthur approached Vincent, who was seated at the middle of a long white cloth-covered table, his back to the wall and looking every inch The Don that he wasn't. Marthur shuffled chairs to sit next to him and greeted him with a kiss on his head.

"Marthur. Glad you changed your mind. Where's Arthur? Is Pete still here?"

"Don't know and yes, Pete's at the bar." As she spoke, Pete walked towards them. The crowd parted and, like a latter-day Moses and the Red Sea, Pete passed through before sitting herself opposite Marthur and raising her glass to Vincent.

"Cheers V. What's with the Georgian doormen in wigs? Have you tried one?"

"Less noticeable than dark suits and the wigs hide the mics better. You never know, it might catch on." At that moment, Beryl appeared and sat next to Marthur, all the time pointing a pocket fan at her neck.

"I don't know where your nephew is Vincent, he's nowhere to be seen." If Vincent's nephew was anything like him, Marthur was relieved he was unable to be found as she was in no mood for work that evening.

"Oh dear, what a shame. I'll meet him soon."

Beryl turned to Marthur with a serious look on her face, put her right arm around Marthur's shoulder and warmly rested her left hand on Marthur's hands on the table. The chip of a diamond engagement ring that Vincent gave her when he was studying laughed on the fingers of Beryl's patting hand. It sparkled between the thin gleaming wedding band and eternity bands, which held boulders of rubies and diamonds. Marthur looked at Beryl's hands then at Beryl's face and wondered what was coming next. Beryl clearly had something to say.

"I know of some lovely cream for your itches Marthur. I've written the name down. You're so brave to be so open about it. Here you are." She passed a note to Marthur. "You'll have to ask for it at the chemist, or… you could pop into the clinic. It's my volunteer reception day on Tuesday, I'll look after you."

Marthur took the folded piece of paper that Beryl had discretely proffered. "Admit what? I'm confused."

As Pete took a mouthful of bubbles, Beryl leaned in closer and pointed under the table.

"Herbs won't do it. You need the big guns."

Pete snorted as she got Beryl's point. Marthur was only just beginning to get the sharp end of it.

"Oh! No! I haven't got it. I just said that to… never mind. Thanks Beryl, I'll remember that." Marthur finished her champagne, Pete stopped choking and they both stood up to say their goodbyes.

"Well Beryl, good luck on V's retirement. I suppose

I'll see you on Thursday as usual, Vincent?"

Marthur held onto Vincent's ears as she had once done when he banged his head on her swing at one of Arthur's parties in the Lakes when she was young. She pulled his head forward, kissed his pate and wiped the lipstick away. Then she kissed Beryl, who wiped the lipstick from her cheek herself. The two friends left the couple, still lovebirds after more than fifty years. Vincent kissed Beryl on her forehead and squeezed his arm tightly around her shoulder. He quickly let go as he spied some business to be done. He left Beryl to point the fan at her neck again. Beryl could see her nephew coming back to the table and stood up, calling to Marthur and Pete, but they seemed not to hear.

"Where did you go to Vincent? She's gone now. I wish you wouldn't keep popping off."

"Oh dear, missed your opportunity again. Not to worry."

Pete set foot on the stairs back up to The Boardroom and Marthur followed.

Vincent didn't like the look of the conversation that his namesake was having at a nearby table. The man had a face that wore many years of trouble, with eyes that looked out for more. Vincent put a hand on his uncle's shoulder and introduced himself. The man didn't stand but simply nodded. Without looking up, he spoke. "You have a choice Vincent. Same as the others."

"Carry on down that path, Harry, and you may be

caught by those shadows that you're so fond of. You're as ganche as that village you live in."

"I'm not the idiot you think I am, Mr O'Sullivan. Be careful now, you know how easily people can go missing. It was so many years ago."

The men stood up. Harry left The Sea. Vincent nodded to one of the doormen, who whispered into his hidden mic to other members of the team, telling them to follow Harry, but Harry was not to be found. As far as they knew, he hadn't left through any door in the building, neither could he be seen moving through any of the secret corridors. They checked all the old hiding places.

"What was all that about? I know him from somewhere."

"That's the reason why you're taking over lad. I've too much to do with another kind of law. Time to put the light on and see what scurries back into the murk."

"Is it your age that makes you talk in riddles Uncle V? I've just paid everyone and now I'm going. I'll pick you up when you call me."

The younger Vincent left The Moon and crossed the road to the carpark behind the council offices. Hopping along the railings of King's Manor and the wall was an enormous beautiful blue-black crow, ringed around one ankle with silver.

Upstairs, The Boardroom was just as full as The Sea. The friends drank champagne and danced with the band sporting their Wayfarer sunglasses. The DJ soon seamlessly took over, supplying wave after infectious wave of throbbing anthemic basslines. The closing twenty minutes began with the haunting Etta James and the floor filled with couples.

"I'm not staying to watch the smoochers. Taxi or walk?"

"Walk. Burt's given me another little bit of gratitude. He's grown it himself, and the park looks lovely at this time of night now they've decorated it with lights."

From the autumn equinox, the council uplit the oldest of the oak, ash, beech, bay, willow and chestnut trees until the start of spring when the trees decorated themselves green and yellow, white and pink again. The friends walked arm in arm along the Chinese lantern strung pathway through the park. Eventually they arrived at the road and set off down the avenue of trees that led up to The Horseshoe from the sideroad. They could see that lights were on all over the house. As they got closer, Frank Zappa rang louder through the air. They looked at each other and groaned in unison. "Arthur's back."

Marthur turned her key, pushed open the door, made her excuses and went upstairs. She could feel the wall that she was about to hit. Zappa finished and Terry set 'angels' loose on the piano in the drawing room.

Champagne corks popped and congratulations chorused as Pete walked into the party. Unnoticed, she filled two 19th century crystal flutes with Mumm, went upstairs and knocked on Marthur's door. The door opened and she handed both glasses to her friend, then headed to her room. Minutes later, she returned to Marthur's room having changed into a pair of men's 1930s Harrods gold silk pyjamas with holly-green piping (a village jumble sale trophy). Her ensemble was finished off by a pair of green pompom pumps.

The fire in Marthur's room gently rippled and popped with the flames licking the back plate. Pete draped herself on the chaise. Marthur made an elaborate curtsey and dutifully handed a glass to the Pierrot-esque Pete.

"You got that fire going quick! I couldn't be bothered. I've just put the heater and electric blanket on in mine."

"It was done for me. I'm being buttered up."

"That's lovely. Just be grateful."

Marthur went into her bathroom, filled the basin with cold water ready for the morning and changed into her flannelettes. Pete stared into the fire, listening to the album Marthur had put on her Technics 1210 deck. She drifted away with the beautiful lilting harmonies that seemed to emanate from the flames as well as the speakers placed on either side of the fireplace. The door to the landing opened slightly. A man's head popped through the gap.

"Sorry, my tonsils are drowning, and I can't wait till the boss is back. It's been a while since I was here last, Vincent said it was up here. Hey… you're listening to the grandparents of reggae! Not many people do that these days."

"That's a bit rude! Three doors along."

The man sheepishly pulled his head back through the door as Marthur came out of her bathroom. She sat on the floor by the fire and lit a joint with a glowing ember that she had picked from the grate with the set of Liberty fire tongs.

"Did I hear someone come in just then?"

"Yes. Vincent's minion. Lost, as people usually are in this TARDIS. Cheeky sod said you were playing granny reggae."

Marthur flipped over the Keith and Enid album on the deck and attempted to talk about the work she had to do the next day, but Pete would have none of it. Then Marthur remembered the letter that Beth had delivered earlier for Pete.

"Beautiful handwriting on the envelope Pete! The Bruins are keeping it in the hall." Keith and Enid ended their performance and Marthur shut the system down.

"Yes, you said earlier, and no, I don't want you to go and get it for me. Thank you."

Then, through a yawn, she mumbled about seeing to it in the morning and went to bed.

Marthur put the guard around the fire, poured herself into bed and she lay like a Sea Star under the heavy wave of the quilt. She gave thanks and floated off to the sound of the party still resonating through the house. Arthur's musical tastes, which were as diverse as his companions, sounded out from the study whenever the door opened.

Terry was freeing all sorts of notes in the drawing room. Band mates from many moons ago were playing along, punctuated by back slapping, laughing and whoops of surprise, shock and delight. All too soon, it was Sunday morning.

Sunday Morning

It was barely light. Despite putting her head under three pillows, she couldn't shut out the tchacking of a pair of jackdaws that were nesting around one of the stacks on the roof. She was sure that they were shouting down the chimney, laughing at her hangover.

In frustration, Marthur threw a pillow in the general direction of the fire, then rolled out of bed and onto her knees. She crawled into the bathroom and laid herself out on the cork floor that was just starting to get warm as the underfloor heating kicked in. Her stomach retched as she unscrewed the toothpaste lid. A rinse with mouthwash was all the attention that her body could take, then she dunked her face in the basin that was now full of freezing water. The hood of her sweatshirt left just enough space to navigate around. Then, less out of consideration for those still sleeping but more for her own safety, Marthur walked gingerly down the stairs. She negotiated a trail full of streamers, balloons, bottles corks and glasses.

The chandelier in the hall sported a collection of shoes that were hung precariously interlocked, like a string of plastic monkeys. She managed to lift her head in time to avoid bringing some, or indeed all of them, crashing down. Tutting ruefully, Marthur opened the door to the study and immediately set about opening the sash windows to allow the fresh misty autumn air to chase away the smells of the party.

Arthur's desk was strewn with even more glasses, plates and ashtrays, but Marthur's desk was unexpectedly clear. She ran her hands over the clean surface in appreciation of her uncle and looked at her captain's chair. He had plumped the cushion under the blanket too. Marthur raised her eyes to the ceiling and promised him a poached egg when he got up.

She removed her laptop from her bag and opened it out on the desk. It felt sticky. Marthur sat down heavily on her chair. There was a loud BANG accompanied by a farting noise! Arthur had replaced the cushion on her chair with a balloon and a whoopie cushion. She gathered her things together and headed for the morning room. It was always clean and fresh in there, no matter what was going on elsewhere in the house.

The comforting smell of coffee and toast that filled the ground floor made her nose twitch, her mouth water and her stomach rumble loudly in anticipation of the taste. Once again, Marthur set the laptop up on the table, switched it on and began typing in her keycode. Almost immediately, it switched itself off and Marthur shouted through the ceiling at her uncle, "And you can forget your bloody egg!"

Marthur plugged the laptop into the socket under the table, wiped the screen and keyboard, and tried to find out more about a non-vegan vegan company that were looking for support. Nothing much came up, which was not necessarily a bad thing, it just meant that she had to dig deeper. She contacted her friend Sally, who was that rare combination of activist, vegan and trouble-shooter. She was exceptional at finding out key information about any organisation or company that one may wish to know about.

Very soon, thanks to Sally's digging, a picture began to emerge. It uncovered a dubiously vegan cosmetics company that were clearly just this side of legal. It was pyramid selling in all but name, but that was not all. Coral Wennal was head of the company that were drawing in the unsuspecting and the susceptible. Basically, anyone who would believe the plastic ambrosia of their carob-coated blurb.

Marthur's brain was hurting. She rested her eye sockets on the heel of her hands. Her long fingers massaged the scalp around her hairline until her head fell forward, hitting the keyboard and deleting the information that she had just uncovered. Marthur realised that she had nodded off and that she may not be ready to work for a while yet. She closed the lid of the computer, plaited her fingers behind her head and rocked on the back legs of her chair, balancing on her toes.

There were signs of movement upstairs. Voices filtered throughout the house. Riffs from Duelling Banjos rang out from Arthur's suite as he opened the door and his leather slippers slapped the stairs as he descended, letting everyone know that he was on the move.

Marthur was composing a refusal for Coral in her head. She had all but edited the swearing, the 'you dids, and the 'when we were seventeen, you made me feel's out of the way and was enjoying simply saying 'no!' when she was distracted by Vincent's car as it pulled around the side of the house. For some reason, she started to feel uneasy and jittery but put it down to her hangover. She sipped on her Nux Vom remedy and continued rocking as Maime let him in.

"Hi, Vincent. You look good this morning. Arthur's around somewhere… try the study. The window on the landing is a good place to try too!"

Maime went into the kitchen while Vincent set off to look for Arthur. Marthur wondered why Maime would send Vincent upstairs to look at a window that he'd seen so many times before. Vincent opened the door to the study, walked over to the French doors, looked out onto the terrace and decided to look elsewhere.

Marthur knew her uncle wasn't in the study and suddenly, growing all too aware of her scruffy apparel, she hoped that the footsteps that were approaching would pass by. She didn't want to see anyone, not even Vincent, although admittedly he had seen her in worse conditions. The footsteps travelled on up the stairs.

The latest housekeeper opened the front door and let herself in the house. Vincent trailed down the staircase and onto the other side of the landing to look through the morning room and to see Maime's apartment. Marthur, still balancing precariously, froze mid-rock when the door behind her opened.

"Sorry to disturb you. Looking for Arthur. He's disappeared again."

Marthur recognised the voice as that of the man who had wanted to find Arthur the previous night. She was glad that her back was to the door. Without turning to face him, she set the chair on its four feet and, internally wishing him gone, suggested he try the study.

Marthur lifted the screen and began typing the letter to Coral that she had already composed in her head. She paused… there was something about his voice that had niggled her. She was dreading meeting any of the other people who may have stayed over.

He closed the door, stood in the middle of the hall and wondered which way to go. He had been in every room in the house except for two bedrooms that were out of bounds and the morning room. He was too scared to risk disturbing the woman at the table again. Arthur must be *somewhere* in this rambling old building. Time was moving on. He had to get this sorted before he went back home, so he took a deep breath and walked into the morning room again.

Marthur started nervously when he opened the door, hiding behind the laptop screen as he walked around the table to the window. He felt intrusive, shy and, for some reason, foolish. He looked out to the other side of the terrace but could not concentrate. Marthur raised her eyes over the top of the screen to look at the man by the window. He was quite scruffy, likely to be one of Arthur's workmen, which for a split second made her feel easier. He spoke. Marthur hid behind her screen again.

"Great views from every window that I've looked

through so far."

Marthur 'mmm'ed in agreement, feeling as ridiculous as she knew that she now looked. She could not bring herself to come out of hiding and remained demoniacally hunched while continuing to type.

In the kitchen, the washing up was underway. Maime was elbow deep in suds at the Belfast sink under the window. Arthur walked into the kitchen and placed a tray of glasses on the island that separated them. The sun shone through the window. It refracted a rainbow of colours through a pelmet of crystal, cannibalised from a broken chandelier of the Raven's days. Maime dried her hands and stood at the other side of the island and the brilliant light behind gave her a halo. She looked every inch the angel that Arthur knew that she was. She reached for the tray but could not raise her eyes to look at Arthur.

"I meant what I said."

"As did I. You know it makes sense." He put a hand on hers and opened his mouth to speak, but Maime cut him off.

"Do we have to talk about it now?"

"After what you said yesterday? I think we do. I don't want you to do it. Anyway, what else is there?"

"Flattering, why didn't you say something before?"

"I could say the same to you. Don't do it Maime."

The new housekeeper broke the atmosphere by walking through the kitchen to the utility room, as if the people in the kitchen were not there. However, she did wonder about the occupants of the house, and on her way back, she refused to go upstairs until the monkey rope of shoes was taken down. Arthur changed the subject.

"Has Marthur surfaced?"

"Just after me."

"Has she started work yet?"

"Not sure, but she shouted a few choice words to you about forgetting your 'bloody egg'."

"That's a shame. I love the way she poaches eggs too!" Arthur opened the door to the study and closed the windows.

Meanwhile in the morning room, Marthur became aware of the smell of ginger that oozed through her pores. She wished that she had braved the shower and cleaned her teeth. She would normally be less concerned as she usually adopted a 'don't give a stuff' attitude for her Sunday appearance. Putting it down to her hangover was no longer working. She could not shake the mismatch of feelings that coursed through her.

A voice in her head told her to collect her things and run from the static that was gathering in the room. A different voice told her not to be so unhospitable and reminded her that she would by now have been making tea and butties for anyone who was working at Heaven. She would have at least offered anyway. In her head, she told the voice that she felt nervous and shy. Nevertheless, she did wonder what his hands were doing in his pockets. Marthur was surprised when she received an answer.

"He's SHY. He's playing with the rubber washers and pinball that he keeps in his work pants."

Marthur stopped typing and looked to her right. It was her mother's voice; she was sure of it. Her hangover was getting worse. Her mother's voice then told her that she shouldn't be shy at her age.

The man at the window struggled to find something to say. He gathered himself to face the scary woman at the table and make conversation. Everything happened at once. The chain of shoes collapsed in the hall accompanied by Arthur's raucous laughter, whilst Pete painted the air of the morning with the colour of her tongue. The cacophony rang through the entire ground floor. It didn't sound good.

"I see you've tried to climb the shoe tree Pete."

Pete replied with one of her looks and set off to the kitchen, picking up her letter from the bears on the way. Arthur opened the door to the morning room.

"Darling!"

Marthur and Vincent turned simultaneously. Vincent smiled at Arthur and his niece scowled at him. In one stride, Arthur wrapped his niece in his arms and patted her head.

"I'm sorry about the balloon, I couldn't resist it. Blame Dr Seuss. You two have introduced yourselves, I take it? Have you been offered a drink?"

They both replied, "No."

"Not to worry, let's go and see where we're going to put this bench then."

Marthur relaxed, no longer caring how she looked. He was just a workman and no one that she knew. Extricating herself from her uncle, she turned to offer coffee and instantly wished that she hadn't. The man at the other side of the table looked at her and she at him. The atmosphere changed again.

"Now then, let me introduce you to Vincent's nephew. He's going to build us a bench or two."

Marthur and Vincent raised an arm, holding out their hands in greeting. A crack of static flew from Marthur's fingers and through Vincent. SHE was standing before him… and in Arthur's house. Was SHE Arthur and Maime's new housekeeper? Or was she with Arthur himself? He would be surprised as she was much closer to his own age than Arthur's. Then again, his greeting had been rather familiar, and she looked like she had just got out of bed. Now he really was confused.

Arthur put the sudden change in atmosphere down to Marthur's hangover and let go of her. He placed his arm around Vincent's shoulders and took him outside. Looking a lot better than she felt, Pete walked into the morning room and found Marthur staring out of the window. Pete sat heavily on one of the sofas; she prepared herself to open the letter.

"So much for you getting down to some work. Fancy some breakfast? I've just met Vincent's nephew and… he isn't a minion."

Marthur didn't reply. Instead, she took the napkin from the folder and handed it to Pete, who put it on the table.

"Give it a rest. Get yourself ready, I'm taking you out."

Pete watched Marthur as she looked down at one of her

little toes that was poking through a hole in her odd sock. Pete followed her eyes as they travelled on up her slouch pants to the blob of sauce that she had failed to wipe away last night. Then Marthur noticed the hot rock holes on her hoodie, finally stopping at the worried expression on Pete's face.

Letting out a cry to God in heaven from her gaping mouth, Marthur ran out of the room, up the staircase and locked herself in her bedroom. She sat on the floor with her back to the door. Pete, confused and a little concerned, followed her friend and eventually Marthur let her in.

"You had better sit down. It's a long story."

"In that case, I'd better get something to sustain us."

Marthur took the lacquered box and showered while Pete brewed some coffee. She returned to find Marthur dressed and looking beautiful. She was sitting cross-legged on the bed clutching an ashtray and a joint that Pete had rolled while she was persuading Marthur to let her in. Marthur lit the joint. Pete sat herself down on the bed opposite Marthur and placed the tray between them. "Come on then. Spill. What's going on Marthur? I think you've got to get whatever it is into perspective."

"Open your letter first."

Pete noted that the look of fear and shock that had swallowed Marthur up not twenty minutes ago had vanished. Marthur was not going to tell her what was going on until the distracting letter was out of the way. For the first time, Pete really studied the envelope.

"Why do you think it's for me?"

"P.H.R. – *Peta Harriet Rowen!*"

"Fair do's, but the paper and ink are definitely as old as the date on it. I don't know anyone who writes like that these days and anyway, it's marked West Riding. Even I know that the Ridings were dissolved when we were nippers. I see why you hadn't noticed all the blatantly obvious indications that the only thing this letter has in common with me is my hair cut."

"Open it."

"No! It feels creepy."

Marthur picked up the letter and reached for the blade she kept on the table by the bed.

"Well, if it's addressed to Raven's Court then as we own the place, it must be ok for us to see what it's all about." Pete took the letter, gently lifting the already peeling flap of the envelope. She read it aloud.

"*'My darling Peter, I write hurriedly from Raven's Cottage. Everything is ready. I leave for Leicester in two days' time to be with my sister. Our aunt has recently died, and the family solicitor is the executor of her last will and testament. Now you are returned from Northumberland, I am making the arrangements to bring you to me. We will be staying with my sister until the estate is settled. We have a house in Banbury. My love, we are free. Nothing else matters. You are alive and we can spend the rest of our days together. Until soon is now, Alice.'* Alice? Who the f is...?"

"Blown if I know, but Peter Raven did."

"Who is Alice indeed. Mystery over, it's most definitely not for me. Right then. I've shared my mystery, now it's your turn, and hurry up because I'm getting hungry."

In the vast garden, Vincent was struggling to focus his concentration on the business at hand. Arthur was suggesting various locations for the benches, but Vincent found it impossible to concentrate.

"Are you ok? You look a bit pale. Did you hit the bottle when you got back with Vincent and Beryl last night?" Arthur noticed Vincent staring at the house. "You had that haunted look a couple of weeks ago."

"No, I stayed dry. Was that your new housekeeper?"

"No. That's my niece... my namesake. She's been my charge since she was nine years old. I thought you'd been introduced."

"No." He wanted to know all about Marthur. He recalled a family party from when he was seven years old. He remembered being introduced to the closest he had come to a faerie who was holding the hand of Arthur's brother in-law. He stroked his right cheek as he remembered that same faerie slapping his face when he had tried to kiss her.

"Marthur was five years old at the time and like a Tasmanian devil when you felt that sting. I thought you'd recognise her. You two might be older and taller, but to me you still look the same." Vincent changed the subject and asked about the yew tree.

"Forget about that. Come on, Vincent O'Sullivan-

Bloxburn, let's go back inside and I'll reintroduce you to my niece."

The Following Autumn

The bride was late. Pete watched from the choir loft while Miss Galpine's fingers danced across the keys introducing the congregation into the church. She played both 'Jesu, Joy of Man's Desiring' and 'Air' from Handel's 'Water Music' three times while the guests congregated in the church. The congregation smiled and bitched whilst they waited for the bride to relieve the pressure from the fidgeting groom at the altar. Was it anticipation or was it fear? Pete could not tell.

Miss Galpine had been St George's church organist for over sixty years. She had witnessed the choir dwindling from a thirty-strong body of basses through to sopranos, to now when there was only the three of them to sing for weddings and funerals. Pete, Beth and Miss Galpine made a good team. As deaf as she was, Miss Galpine was a perfect accompanist. She followed the vibrations from the organ that she had come to know so well over the years. She sensed the spirit and emotion in the air along with the voices of her singers rather than the dots on the page.

Miss Galpine could not see into the church below but her years of playing such gigs had trained her ears to recognise what was happening away from the choir loft. Today, her sixth sense kicked in as she played Pachelbel's 'Canon in D'. The wedding guests hushed as the flower girls littered the aisle with rose petals. Pete looked over to the presbytery door and watched one of the cleaners, in her pristine nylon tabard, shaking her head at the thought of scraping the sticky mush of petals off the tiles when everyone had gone.

As the flower girls seated themselves either side of the altar gates, Miss Galpine introduced Schubert's 'Ave Maria'. Pete opened her mouth to hail the entrance of the bride. Miss Galpine chuckled to herself as Pete's timbre told her of the frozen expression on the face of the bridegroom as his bride-to-be oozed up the aisle. Miss Galpine heard Pete draw a hesitant breath a fraction too early and prepared herself to pick her up four bars along in Schubert's melody.

She knew the bride would be a quarter of the way down the aisle by now and, though she kept the note clean, Miss Galpine recognised that Pete had not the breath left in her vocal cords. Just as she thought, Pete's voice cracked right at the end of the verse. Miss Galpine extended the intro to the second half whilst Pete composed herself for the last run.

The last wedding that Pete had sang at was Arthur and Maime's handfasting ceremony. Of the few weddings that she had attended as a guest, she had never before seen such a look of horror on a groom's face. This was not what she had expected to see or feel. She found herself singing for the groom alone as he looked up into the rafters that were like the skeleton of a ship. He closed his eyes and his lips moved in prayer to take him into the safety of the upturned ark that he was standing under, hoping to be saved from the destroying flood on its way to meet him.

Mater Dei

Ora pro nobis peccatoribus

Nunc et in hora mortis

In hora mortis nostrae

In hora mortis, mortis nostrae

In hora mortis nostrae

Ave Maria.

Miss Galpine smiled. She knew what the groom was thinking. 'Mother of God, pray for us at the hour of our death'.

Pete, long-limbed and slim, seated herself on the bench next to the short and stocky Miss Galpine, resplendent in a kilt and pale pink blouse, who was now thumbing her way through the yellowing ancient sheet music for Psalm 23. She set the sheets in front of her, even though she played with her eyes closed, then leaned over to whisper in Pete's ear.

"Didn't Beth warn you not to look when the bride walks in? I'll give it two."

"Two years?"

"Two *hours* after communion, judging by the gasp you let out as the bride walked up the aisle. Where's Beth?"

A man and woman were employed to stand in front of the altar, face the guests and strike up with all the verses of 'Respect' twice over with a guitar solo in between. They followed this with 'Love Will Keep Us Together'.

As Miss Galpine cringed along with the strumming, Pete crept down the worn steps and went outside. Beth was sitting on the wall preparing a reefer.

"Ey up lass, we're on in a bit."

"I watched her pull up, I couldn't face it. I'm not fond of great songs being played in that awful happy-clappy way at mass. I noticed Miss G extending the bit before you came in again, so I gathered you were watching as the bride glooped in. I did suggest that you shouldn't watch."

"It was just the way his face changed. He didn't recognise the woman he's been waking up with for the past however many mornings."

"Mmm. As if the groom were looking at a stranger." Beth had seen the look many times herself from the balcony of the loft. Nervous, hopeful for the future, excited? All these things perhaps, but there is often a brief moment of recognition. The woman they turned to watch walking up the aisle was not the woman that they had proposed to.

In the twenty-four hours since their fluttering hearts had kissed goodbye, the woman who fed his joy, desire and passion for the future had been replaced by a doppelganger wearing a buttermilk Edwardian riding habit and flanked by two other women in puce Bo Peep dresses. They were looking at him and grinning on a side of their faces that he had never seen before.

The duo finished and Pete crept back up the stairs with Beth as the couple publicly declared their undying love. Beth whispered in Pete's ear.

"He can't even look at her while he's saying his vows. He looks terrified, not ecstatic. Poor sod."

"What about her when she realises that *she* wants out?"

"Yes, it happens with brides too, but I only see their expressions when I'm doing a reading or when they're walking away from the altar. People get so caught up in the trappings, their desire to be wed, more than their desire to be with the right person for the rest of their hopefully happy and long lives. Weddings like this take an age to plan and they cost a fortune too. By this point, they're too afraid to back out. If she had shown that side of her style and personality, before he had committed, there would be no wedding. But then, of course, we would not be taking home seventy pounds each for the pleasure of singing beautiful tunes with Groover Galpine. I'll give it two years."

"Maybe he thinks he should be committed for marrying."

Miss Galpine coughed, giving the cue for Beth and Pete as the priest announced the signing of the register.

'The Lord's My Shepherd, I'll Not Want' was the only request, but Miss Galpine recognised the signs of trouble brewing between the families below the loft. Puccini's 'Flower Duet' and 'Panis Angelicus' later, the ushers had managed to subdue the divide, and the priest, registrar and the couple emerged from the sacristy. Miss Galpine played 'Wind Beneath My Wings'.

Beth and Pete watched on as a smug bride almost

skipped down the aisle pulling a reluctant husband along. He looked back in a silent plea to be rescued by the best man walking just behind his new wife. All the best man could do was shrug his shoulders, shake his head and smile unconvincingly as he escorted one of the puce Bo Peeps out of the church and into the hail of confetti and rice.

Once the remaining guests had begun leaving their pews, the cleaners crept out of the presbytery and sidled along the wall under the stations of the cross. They stood at the top of the aisles, ready to sweep through and herd the stragglers to the door with their mops and buckets, scrapers at the ready. They made no secret of their disdain for the choice of music, muttering about the dire consequences of a mixed marriage and how standards were slipping in the church as a body.

Beth's fellow wedding players had gone. She side-stepped down the narrow spiral stairs to say her goodbyes but found that she was alone.

Once they had shooed the last of the guests out, the cleaners swept through like ninjas. Unseen, largely unheard and always swift. They even managed to remove the plastic flowers from the ends of every other pew and the bruised rose petals that were stuck to the tiled floor.

Beth stood on the same foot-worn step that her mother had stood upon when locking the door to the choir loft. She remembered the story of her father's proposal to her mother. The only chap that had ever spoken to Beth on the choir loft steps was a six-foot-seven traveller after she had sung at a funeral. He had thrust a hundred pounds into her hand and told her that she had been the only person to make him cry in twenty years.

The church was dark. The sanctuary lamp and the candles at the altars to the Blessed Virgin and the Sacred Heart were the only remaining pockets of light. Beth headed for the presbytery. As she walked under the Stations of the Cross, she noticed shining balls of iridescence floating around the aisles. This was not unusual in St George's. As she walked back through the church, one of the balls turned from pale yellow to a vibrant electric blue. Beth lit her candles at the Lady Chapel, offering up the light to guide the soul passing over.

Beth left through the presbytery and lengthened her stride. As she turned onto the main street, she heard someone calling her name. She looked up and saw a man standing by the gate to the graveyard that, legend would have it, was the final resting place of Dick Turpin and his horse. The man waved to her and doffed his trilby as Beth waved and walked quickly past.

She caught up with Miss Galpine and Pete as they walked arm in arm to The Phoenix, a tiny pub inside George Street Bar. They were going to discuss over a noggin of rum the dazed expression of the groom as his wife had led him out of the church barking orders at both him and the guests.

"Why do you think I've stayed single? You shouldn't marry just anyone you know."

Miss Galpine had been due to marry. After a rehearsal in Miss Galpine's house one evening years ago, she had showed Beth the delicate silk-satin wedding dress that hung on a padded hanger on her wardrobe door, just as it had been left the night before her wedding day. The dress was tiny. Elegant, cut on the cross and panelled with delicate English lace. It had Vandyke sleeves that were finished with a perfect pearl at the finger band.

"Was he a smart man, your fiancé, Miss G?" Miss Galpine looked at Beth and grinned.

"My fiancé was a conscientious objector. He died from the beatings that he received in town for refusing to go to war. It was the night before we were due to marry. I never met anyone else, no one matched up. He was a peaceful vegetarian and spent his life in corduroy and overalls. He was an artist. He had long hair, smoked a chillum of that stuff you pair do and did amazing things with his hands!" Miss Galpine glowed, Pete blushed crimson and Beth chuckled as the rum melted Miss G's reserve. The wrinkles on Miss Galpine's face disappeared and the sadness left her brow. Her cheeks swelled as she talked of her bohemian lover.

"He used to paint me nude y'know. Pete, your face is the same colour as your scarf. You don't stop thinking about it when you get older y'know, even if you don't get the opportunity, especially if it was good."

The head cleaner arrived and joined in with the conversation. "They think sex was invented when they were sixteen Mable, and that we know nothing of passion." The cleaner grinned at Miss Galpine.

Beth bought another rum for both Miss Galpine and the cleaner, leaving them to discuss the bride's dress.

"It was obviously not one of Mavis & Lisa Originals' designs, she would *never* let a dress like that leave her shop."

"The things you find out about people. She was a bit of a goer by the sounds of it."

"I suppose nothing changes except the fashions and your hair."

"That was on the radio this morning."

"She was right about the dress though."

End of Book 1

The closer you get to the top of the
Old Man by Coniston Water, the
narrower and steeper it becomes.
Patience, hardy sticks and boots,
make it easier to get there.
Final thanks at the top of the hill
to She who listens well, another
protector of the Holy Grail.
Onwards.

Looking For The Last Piece: Book 2 –
Until Soon is Now

Meanwhile in the North

Until the middle of the 1960s, the tiny cluster of homestead dwellings and farms under the name of Ganche Lin, was too small to register on any map other than on old Ordinance Survey cartography. Situated at one end of the cross of the road facing east and west, stood a 12th century church. At the other, a pool of water, fabled to be a former ducking site, sat deep, black and cold. The road north led to the ruins of a castle on top of the hill and the south fork led directly to the valley floor. Ganche Lin's obscurity changed with the disappearance of Vincent O'Sullivan's nephew. The unwelcome publicity lifted a veil to the outside world.

These days, the secluded hamlet boasted a combined public house, local shop, post office and doctor's surgery and, thanks to the all-encompassing internet and its gift of exposure, Ganche Lin's reputation had grown as a spot of great beauty.

As one season melded into another, hikers came for the panoramic views from the top of the hill and mountain bikers for the dangerous terrain on the way down to the bottom. Fossil hunters and folklorists turned up in greater numbers to catch a glimpse of the peculiarities of the village, and twitchers came for the rare sightings and reputedly uncommon behaviour of otherwise common birds in that particular area, proving the 'birds of a feather' age-old saying obsolete... *To be published in early 2023*